A Novel Christmas

Stacey Broadbent

Published by Stacey Broadbent, Ashburton, NZ

Proofreading by Spell Bound
Cover image from Deposit Photos
Cover Design by Stacey Broadbent

ISBN: 978-0-473-77128-7 (paperback)
         978-0-473-77129-4 (kindle)

A Novel Christmas

Stacey Broadbent

Dedicated to

The crew and patrons of Te Kete Tuhinga Ashburton
Library, who not only inspired this story, but provided a
space for me to feel I truly belong.

Author's Note

This story is set in New Zealand, in a small town called Ashburton, which is in the area of Mid Canterbury. In New Zealand, we use UK spelling and terms you may be unfamiliar with. Please remember these are not errors, it's just the way we do things here.

Chapter One

"Tay, it's not healthy to squirrel yourself away like this." Lynette stands with her hip cocked as she eyes Taylor's attire. "It's two in the afternoon and you're sitting there in your pyjamas still."

Taylor shrugs. "They're comfy. And sitting at a desk for eight hours a day requires comfort."

Lynette levels her with a stare. "That's exactly what I'm talking about. You shut yourself off from the world like some old spinster."

Taylor quirks a brow. "I'm not shut off. I have you. And Atticus." She gives Atticus a scratch under the chin, leaning back in triumph.

"Your cat doesn't count, and neither do I. You need to get out and meet people, boo."

"I'm perfectly content here in my office, with all my books, thank you very much." She waves an arm around the room. "In case you've forgotten, Lynny, I'm under contract to release two books a year, and right now I'm staring down the barrel of a looming deadline, and I'm nowhere near where I need to be." She turns back to her screen with the ever-present blinking cursor, reminding her she's fresh out of ideas.

"Uh-huh. And how's that going for you?" Lynette leans down, squinting at the wordcount, which Taylor quickly covers up. "Correct me if I'm wrong, but novels are usually longer than three thousand words." She waves a manicured finger in the air.

A groan escapes Taylor's lips, and she crumples forward, resting her forehead on her hands. "I know, okay? But that's exactly why I can't go out with you. How can I when I have so much to do?"

Lynette drags a chair across the floor, leaving scuff marks on the rug as she does. "Listen." She spins her around, taking hold of her hands on either side of Atticus's head. "I know you've got a lot on your plate, but I honestly think you're burned out. You need a break." She nods towards the blank screen. "You've been staring at that for far too long. It's not good for you."

"I mean, that's not entirely true. It pays the bills, gives me money to play with."

"Which would be great if you actually went out and used some of it every now and again. What good is money if you don't go anywhere?"

"Security?" She means it to sound confident, but instead it ends up sounding like a question.

"Babe, you're thirty not seventy. Live a little, have some fun while you're still young enough to enjoy it."

She does have a point, not that Taylor wants to admit that to her. She can't remember the last time she went out and had fun. For that matter, she can't remember the last time writing felt like fun instead of a chore. That was never what it was meant to be.

"Come on. It's one hour of your life. I really think you'll enjoy it." Lynette's lips curl into a grin. "And if it helps, the librarian is easy on the eyes too," she says in a sing song voice.

"Oh no." Taylor shakes her head. "You're not fixing me up with someone. I'm not doing that again."

"What? I have impeccable taste in men."

She snorts. "That's not the word I would choose to describe it. Need I remind you of the judo guy who looked like he was wearing a jumper even when he wasn't?"

Lynette holds up a finger. "In my defence, I had never seen him shirtless before. How was I meant to know?"

"You could see it out the top of his collar! *And* he was a stage four cling-on. I couldn't pee without him following me." She shakes her head again. "No thank you."

"Okay, but that was one guy."

Taylor simply raises an eyebrow.

"Okay, so my track record isn't that great, but I'm telling you, you'll love Brodie."

"Because he's a librarian and I write books? I hate to break it to you, but that does not a relationship make, my friend."

"No, but it's a start. He's seriously cute, reads so much he could rival you, and he's creative too. I've been to some of the art classes he takes, and the guy has talent."

If she's honest, he does sound like the kind of guy she'd like, but it's not like she has time for a relationship right now. She has one month to get this manuscript finished and polished before it goes to the publisher, and right now the words are dried up. There's nothing left in the tank. No big idea, no plot twist in mind, not even a title. Just three thousand words of drivel.

"Come on. Just come once and see what you think. I promise I won't make you come again if you really don't enjoy it. But... I know you will. They're my kind of people, and I'm *your* kind of people, so that makes them *our* kind of people."

She can't argue with that logic. "I guess it couldn't hurt to go out for an hour." Taylor holds up a finger, which Atticus kindly bats. "But only one hour, then I have to get back to this."

Lynette lets out an excited squee and practically bounces in her seat. "You'll see, this will be the best thing to happen to you."

I don't know that I'd go that far, Taylor thinks, *but at the very least, it might give me some fodder for the book.*

"Who knows? Maybe I'll be inspired or find my next muse."

"Atta girl."

Chapter Two

"Are you sure about this?" Taylor pulls Lynette aside, letting the old gentleman behind them pass. What seemed like a good idea at home, now seems like a monumental mistake. There are people everywhere. "It feels rude to just show up."

"God, Tay, you're such a worrywart. I've been coming for months, and they've not turned anyone away so far." She takes hold of her hand and drags her through the sliding doors. "Come on. We've made it this far. Only a few more metres."

The library is a hub of sound as they pass the café, complete with Christmas decals on the windows even though it's only November. They carry on through to an open space with tiered seating. On the ground level is a small circle of chairs, a trolley stacked with books, and a sign that reads "Welcome to Book Club". A man with chestnut hair that flops into his eyes stands to one side. He has broad shoulders and a slim waist, and damn if he doesn't fill out those jeans. But of all things to be wearing, he chooses a Christmas shirt. In November. Blasphemy. Anything Christmas belongs in December. *Late* December. No earlier.

"Lynette, I see you've brought a friend with you. That's great," he says, ushering them towards the centre, but not before giving Taylor what can only be described as a panty-dropping smile. *Goddamn.*

"If you'd just like to write your name on a tag then find a seat, we'll be getting started in a few minutes.

Taylor grabs the sharpie from the table and scrawls her name, adding petals around the 'o' to make a flower as she's done since she could spell her own name. She unpeels the tag and sticks it to her t-shirt while Lynette does the same. They each take a seat.

"See? He's cute, right?" Lynette whispers behind her hand, nodding her head towards the man who must be the infamous Brodie.

"Oh my God, shush! He'll hear you." Taylor's voice comes out louder than she means it to be, and the librarian glances her way with a questioning smile. She slides further down into her seat, willing it to swallow her whole. *How did I used to do this every day?*

Lynette stifles a laugh. "You dork. Now he definitely knows we're talking about him."

The librarian clears his throat, his cheeks flushed. "All right, shall we get started?" Conversations slowly peter out, and everyone turns their attention to him. "I see we have some new faces joining us today, so how about we start by doing a quick introduction around the circle? I'll start us off." He holds up his lanyard with an ID card. "I'm Brodie, and I'm the Community Librarian." He gestures to the woman beside him.

She offers a small wave. "I'm Sue, ex-teacher and principal."

"Jai," says a man as he unclips his helmet and runs a hand through his unkempt hair.

"Hi, I'm Jocelyn."

"Vera."

"I'm Rowena. I write for the paper."

"I'm Dom."

"Hi everyone, I'm Chrissie."

"I'm Helen, like Helen of Troy," says a bolshy older woman with cropped silver hair and a glint in her eye. "And can I say, you've got a lovely crop of hair. Is that your natural colour?" She raises her brows at Taylor, who lets out a strangled cough.

"Oh, ah, no." She touches a hand to her short copper locks. "I change my hair colour all the time. Trying something different."

"Well, it suits you. Reminds me of a cavalier I once had. Oh, he was a dashing pup."

"Um, thanks?" Taylor gives Lynette a side-eye, and she snorts.

"Totally calling you Cav now."

"Look, you've gone and embarrassed the poor girl," Vera says. "You look lovely, dear."

"Yes, you do. Makes you seem bright and sunny, like a ray of sunshine." A tall man with a thick mane of hair and the beginnings of a five o'clock shadow dusting his chin gives a wave. "I'm Byron."

"I think you know who I am." Lynette pokes her tongue out.

"Ah, and I'm Taylor." She raises a hand in a wave, sure her cheeks are bright red as the librarian's eyes land on her for a brief moment.

"Welcome to Book Club, it's always great to have new people joining in." Brodie slaps his hands against his thighs. "Chrissie, would you like to start us off? For those of you who are new, we'll pass around this notebook for you to write down your recommendations for the month." He hands the pad and pen to Chrissie then sits back.

"I had a slow reading month. I think I'm in a bit of a slump because nothing seems to be grabbing me. I've started I think five different books, and they're all partially read but not finished."

Brodie nods, and a strand of hair attaches itself to his long lashes. Another one of those lucky men graced with what every woman on earth desires. "Mmm, I hate when that happens. There's no shame in putting a book away for another day or not picking it up again though. Remember, not every book will be to everyone's liking."

He's got that right. Writing to market was never really Taylor's thing, but she tried to write what the people wanted. That being said, she still remembers the first time she received a scathing review on one of her books. It just about broke her. 99% of reviews are positive, but you get one that's not, and that's the one that sears into your memory. That's the one you'll recall at 2am when you can't sleep. She learned not to read reviews after that.

"Yes, but I do feel guilty not finishing them. I mean, someone has put all that effort into writing it."

"Pfft, nope. Life is too short to read books you're not enjoying." Lynette folds her arms across her chest. "If it doesn't grab me within the first chapter or two, I'm putting that bad boy aside."

Taylor casts her a sidewards glance, and she grins back. Best friends they may be, but reading a book to the very end is where they differ. Taylor's a serial read-it-till-it's-done kind of girl, and Lynette's a I-don't-have-time-for-this reader. Case and point, she is the first person to read everything Taylor writes, and while she loves her stories, once Taylor started dabbling in the spicier side of things, Lynette couldn't do it anymore. She said it was too weird reading sex from her point of view. There are some things friends just don't need to know about each other. Not that Taylor's sex life is anything to write home about. Far from it, in fact. She just happens to have a *very* active imagination.

"But do you come back to it later?" Chrissie asks.

Lynette shrugs. "Depends on the book. Or the format. Like sometimes I can't get into the physical book, but the audio will have me captivated."

"Oh, I hadn't thought of that. I might have to try an audiobook next time. I did manage to find one that stuck. Local author too. One of my friends read it and passed it on." She holds up a book with a gentleman carrying a woman in his arms. "It's called *Shadows of Humiliation* by Deborah Carter. It's a historical romance with a twist. I really felt like I was in their world, you know? Loved it."

"Oh nice. I might have to see if we can get a copy for the library. We like to support our local authors when we can." Brodie jots down the title on a piece of paper.

"Oh, you should. I think a lot of people would like it. She's got other books too."

"It does sound right up my alley." Vera opens her diary and makes a note.

"Excellent, thanks, Chrissie." Brodie smiles. "Jai, what do you have for us today?"

He pulls his backpack up onto his lap and rifles through the contents. "Ah, I read this one." He holds up a tattered copy of *The Great Gatsby* by F. Scott Fitzgerald. "I'm trying to read a classic every month."

"Oh, I do love the classics. Isn't it a fabulous read?" Rowena leans forward, pushing her red-rimmed glasses further onto the bridge of her nose.

Jai's brow furrows. "Um, I'm not sure that I liked it all that much. The people are… not likeable."

"It's just about a bunch of rich folks having a party, isn't it?" Lynette asks, and Rowena gasps as if the very thread of her existence is being called into question.

"It's so much more than that. It's a tragic love story about one man's obsession with a married woman."

Lynette whistles low. "Yikes. Not my bag, sorry."

"I didn't really enjoy it either," Jai admits.

Brodie laughs. "Some of the classics do tend to be polarising."

"The movie isn't half bad though," Helen pipes up. "That Leonardo fellow is quite dashing, isn't he?"

"I wouldn't kick him out of bed," Lynette says with a devilish grin. Byron chuckles, and a few of the women titter. Lynette has never been one to mince words. She'll call a spade a spade, and she doesn't care what anyone else thinks. It's one of the things Taylor loves about her, unless, of course, it involves dragging her out of her comfort zone or calling her out in front of a cute guy.

Brodie clears his throat, trying to get the topic back on track. "Jocelyn, any five star reads this month?"

She proceeds to pull out three books and give an in-depth retelling of each one and her thoughts on them. Before she's even finished, people are asking if they can read them next. The whole book club has the air of a swap meet, where everyone shows off what they have, and others race to see who gets it first. Taylor's loathe to admit that Lynette may have been right. These *are* her kind of people, and she's already feeling a buzz of energy in her chest. She needed this. Being cooped up in her office day in and day out doesn't offer much in inspiration, unlike this pot of gold right here.

"I read this one." Dom holds up a copy of the latest James Patterson book, which sparks off an in-depth conversation about how frequently he releases books.

Helen has everyone in fits of laughter as she holds up a spicy therian romance and tells us how she's learned a thing or two from them. "If I'd found these when I was younger, I tell you." She fans her face. She's also quick to nab a book that one of the others describes as 'saucy and thrilling'.

"I've been reading up about fungi and how to forage for them in nature," Byron says next. "Yeah, I'm really enjoying the process, eh? It really makes me happy to be out in the world, enjoying the bounty that Mother Nature provides us. It's cathartic."

"So you've actually gone out and found some in the wild?" Vera asks, and Byron nods. "And you've eaten them?" He nods again. "You're game."

He chuckles. "Yeah, I guess, but I was super careful. I've been out a few times now." He holds his hands up, palms out. "I'm still here, so I must be doing it right." He laughs, running his hand through his hair. "It's really freeing. I recommend it to everyone. And this book is great." He holds it aloft, but there are no takers on that one. Not everyone is keen to try their luck, but it does sow the seed of an idea in Taylor's mind.

"I might take it, actually." She smiles, reaching forward. Lynette gives her an odd stare, mouthing the word 'fungus' at her. Taylor stuffs the book into her bag. "Research."

Lynette pulls out her phone, though she keeps her eye on Taylor, as if worried she's about to turn into a fungus just by taking the book. She opens her reading journal app then quickly forgets about her best friend as a cheeky grin spreads across her face. "Well, I've got some juicy ones for you, Helen." She gives an exaggerated wink. "I read one by Nicole S. Goodin, another kiwi." She glances up at Chrissie. "It's called *The First Rule*, and it has twin brothers," she sing-songs with a little wiggle in her seat.

"Oh no." Helen screws up her nose. "I like them spicy, but I'm not into incest."

Brodie seems to choke on air. He covers his mouth with his hand, coughing, and Taylor can't help but notice a smudge of paint across his knuckles and the back of his hand.

"Eww that is absolutely *not* what I meant, Helen." Lynette shudders, then the corners of her mouth pull up into a grin. "They're not tag teaming her. She's with them at separate times."

"I'm not sure that's any better," Sue quips.

"Trust me, it is. It's *everything*." Lynette scrolls further down her phone. "Let's see, what else?" She taps a finger against her chin, then glances around the circle before putting her phone away. "You know what? I don't think these other ones are for here. They're a little on the darker side."

"Oh, I don't know. I do love a good thriller." A woman leans forward, her nametag barely hanging on. "A bit of whodunnit really gets the heart racing." That's not the kind of *dark* Lynette is talking about, though it *will* raise the heart rate. Taylor hasn't been game enough to read any of the really dark ones, but from what Lynette tells her, they're like if Stephen King took over writing a Tessa Bailey book—dark, twisted, and a whole lot of spice. In fact, spice might not even be the right word for it. It's too vanilla for the things Lynette has let slip. Raw, unbridled... and disturbing maybe, terrifying even. That sounds more like it. The very thought of reading one of them is enough to give Taylor nightmares, and yet, she's tempted to see what all the fuss is about.

Brodie clears his throat, bringing her back to the present. "And what about you, Taylor? What have you been reading this month?" He smiles, and tiny crinkles form at the corner of his eyes. There's something so inviting about that. Makes him seem kind and approachable.

"Tay," Lynette prompts.

"Oh, um." She tears her eyes away from Brodie's and fumbles with the book in her hand. "Sorry, I was away with the fairies."

"The mind of a writer, am I right? She probably hasn't read much lately, have you, Tay? Too busy working on your own book," Lynette pipes up with a shit-eating grin. If there wasn't a room full of people, Taylor would kill her right here, right now. She deliberately writes under a nom-de-plume, so people don't associate her with her books. Even her family don't know what she does, and that's the way she likes it. Anonymous.

"You're an author?" Brodie asks with interest.

"I… uh…"

"Yes, she is. She's written, what is it now? Six books? Seven?" Lynette asks, her cheshire smile suggesting she's feeling rather smug with herself. If Taylor had known this was her plan, she never would've let her drag her out of the house.

"Eight." Her answer is stilted as she tries not to scowl in her direction. Lynette simply winks, as if it's all fun and games, as if it is all part of the plan. Just not one Taylor is privy to.

"An author? How wonderful." Rowena lowers her glasses. "Are they in the library?" She looks to Brodie, as if he hasn't just found out the very same information as her.

"I'm not sure." He turns back to Taylor. "Do you write under your own name?" His eyes dart to the side, and she can see he's mentally scrolling through the authors he knows who have the name Taylor.

"No, I don't. I like to keep it separate from my personal life." She offers him a smile that she hopes conveys the need to drop the subject.

"Oh but you could tell us. We wouldn't tell anyone, would we, ladies? Ah, and gentlemen?" Helen glances around the room. "We must be the exception to the rule, surely, as your fellow book club members."

Lynette stifles a laugh behind her hand, and Taylor stares, open mouthed. She barely knows anything about these people, except their reading tastes, and that is not enough for her to trust them with something so private as her pen name.

"Maybe another time?" Taylor suggests, quietly seething inside. "Once I've gotten to know you all a bit better, perhaps," she lies through the skin of her teeth, because there is no way in hell she's coming back here ever again.

Chapter three

"Not cool, man." Taylor folds her arms across her chest as Lynette slides into the driver's seat and pulls the car door closed behind her.

"Oh come on, it was all in fun."

"You outed me! You know how I feel about people being in my business."

"Tay, I love you, but you need to stop holding onto that. Not everyone is like Jeremy."

Taylor shoots her a warning glare. Lynette knows the rules. His name does not get spoken aloud. Ever.

She holds her hands up in placation. "Sorry, sorry." She zips her finger and thumb across her lips. "I shouldn't have said his name. Put that aside though. Did you not hear how excited they were to find out you're a writer?"

"Of course I did, and that's exactly how it starts."

She rolls her eyes, which only tightens Taylor's chest further. She rubs a hand against her breastbone, as if she can massage away the pain.

"Come on, they're not like that. You know you have to move on from what... *he*... did at some point, right? You can't keep using it as an excuse to push people away."

"I'm not pushing anyone away."

She quirks her brow. "Go and ask Brodie out then."

Taylor gives her a pointed stare. "Just because I don't want to ask a stranger out on a date, doesn't mean I'm pushing them away. Besides, I don't need a man to be happy."

"I know you say that, but..."

She holds up a finger. "I *do* mean it. I'm fine, Lynny."

"But you're not though." She turns in her seat. "He hurt you; I get it. And I'm not even going to pretend to understand how you feel, because I know it won't even come close to reality, but—" She breaks off, and her eyes soften. "I worry about you, okay? And I don't just mean because you won't get back on the proverbial wagon and go out on a date, but because you've stopped living, Tay. It makes me sad to see you avoiding life."

"I'm not avoiding life." The words come out of Taylor's mouth, but they don't sound genuine, even to her own ears. She huffs out a sigh. "I'm not *trying* to avoid life, anyway."

"Maybe not, but you're not actively engaging with it either. I don't care that you're not dating, but I *do* care that you're not getting amongst it like you used to. Where did my effervescent friend go? The one who was always up for a challenge or to meet new people? Because I haven't seen her in a long time."

Jesus. Tell me how you really feel. Taylor has to look away before the tears that prick her eyes let loose. She knows she's changed. She's not the same person she used to be, but that's what happens when you get burned by someone you thought loved you. She's not the social butterfly anymore because she can't risk going through that again. Being vulnerable is too hard, too risky. And anyway, she gets the same stimulation from her characters as she ever did at a party. Is it any wonder she'd rather be curled up on her reading chair with a good book and a cup of coffee instead of gallivanting around? Who has the time and energy for that kind of carry on after thirty? Taylor certainly doesn't. And she's perfectly fine with that.

Just… fine.

"Tay?" Lynette reaches for her hand, and that's all it takes.

Goddamn it.

Taylor sniffs, but it's not enough to stop the tear from welling up and trickling down her cheek. Okay, so maybe she's not as fine as she thought she was.

"Is this like an intervention or something?" She attempts to smile through her tears.

"I mean, maybe?" Lynette grins. "Honestly though, I didn't set out to upset you. You know that, right?"

"I know."

"Hot librarian aside, I only want you to be happy. You don't have to date, but I *do* think you need to start coming out more. Even if it's just once a week. We can do something together, out in the open, where there are people."

Taylor frowns, and Lynette chuckles. "They're not all that bad. You used to like people, remember?"

"I guess."

"You have to learn to trust again. I promise, I won't out you again if you promise to make an effort to be more present in the world." She quirks a brow at her. "Deal?"

The idea of being vulnerable around people again is terrifying, but anyone can see how much this means to her, and, if she's honest, Taylor thinks she's right. The tears cascading down her face are proof of that.

She swipes a hand across both cheeks and sniffs. "Okay, I promise. But no setting me up with anyone, alright? Brodie seems nice and all, but I'm still not ready for any of that."

Lynette purses her lips, scrunching her nose up. "I think you're wrong, but if that's what it will take to get you out of that stuffy office once in a while, then I'll take it."

Chapter four

For the first time in what feels like ages, the words are flowing from Taylor's fingertips. She's been home from her outing with Lynnette for a little over three hours and already she's managed to double her wordcount.

The book of fungi, open to the chart of poisonous types to avoid, sits beside her. Inspired by Byron's foray into the world of foraging, she's made a plan for her FMC to do something similar, only she won't be as lucky when she stumbles across an unsuspecting looking one that turns out to be toxic.

Taylor leans back in her seat, looking back over the screeds of words.

I hate that Lynette was right.

But I love that I've got my mojo back.

Atticus unfolds himself from Taylor's lap and stretches, his claws digging into her thighs.

Taylor inhales sharply. "I love you too, but please don't. These are my favourite writing pyjamas." With one hand stroking Atticus's head, she wedges the other between his claws and her threadbare pants, trying to unhook them before he leaves any damage. The business that sold them closed a year ago and she can't get any more, so these are as precious as gold. You need to be comfortable to be creative, and in the world of pants… nothing compares to these ones.

With a swish of his tail, Atticus butts his head against Taylor's hand then leaps from her lap to the desktop, narrowly missing the top of the keyboard and the delete button. He makes himself at home, curling into a ball across the open page of the fungi book, and closing his eyes, effectively putting an end to Taylor's research. Everyone knows you can't disturb a cat once it's settled. It's probably time for a coffee break anyway.

She pushes back from her desk, stretching her arms above her head and twisting her neck side-to-side, then wiggling each finger in turn. After a friend wound up with RSI from not taking breaks, she made it a top priority to do regular stretches. People think writing is a sedentary job, but the way Taylor sees it, it's like a workout for your mind and your spirit, and it can take a toll on the body. Of course, allowing herself to wallow away from the world probably wasn't that great for her mind and spirit either.

In the kitchen, she rests a hip against the counter while she waits for the jug to boil. Her stomach grumbles, reminding her she's not eaten since earlier that morning, and it's now somewhere after eight. The fridge holds little more than half a bottle of milk with the best before date of two days prior, a chunk of cheese, and various condiments. Nothing substantial or appetising. The cupboards don't offer up much more because, unlike every other week, she was at book club instead of doing her online grocery order.

With one last longing look at the bare fridge, she swipes her keys from the counter and slips her feet into a pair of ballet flats. The fish and chip shop on the corner will still be open, and that will have to do. Not exactly the meal of champions, but needs must, and right now, her stomach is telling her it is a dire need.

Pulling her cardi tight to her chest, she walks with pace, keeping one eye on her surroundings, and the other firmly on the lit-up store down the road. It is 100 metres at most, but Taylor has never been a fan of the dark, even the hazy dim of dusk that lasts forever on a summer's evening is too dark for her. She's put it down to the time she'd been at a friend's for a sleepover at the age of six or seven, and her friend's older brother put the movie *Poltergeist* on. It had terrified her, and she'd not been able to sleep without a light on ever since. Twenty-odd years later and she still can't walk the street at night without her heart pounding in her chest.

She rounds the corner and heaves a sigh of relief as she's basked in fluorescent light from the chip shop windows. It's still warm out, so they have the double doors wide open, and the hum of music that sounds suspiciously like Christmas carols flows from the overhead speakers. They've already got their windows sprayed with fake snow and holly. Retail stores seem to push it earlier and earlier each year.

Still, her stomach is about to eat itself, so Taylor lopes towards the counter, her eyes fixed on the menu board. She's so preoccupied, she doesn't notice the man standing at the counter until he turns with his bundle of fish and chips and almost bowls her over.

"Oh shit," he says, juggling his food parcel so it doesn't slip from his arms. "Sorry, I didn't see you there. Are you okay?"

Taylor keeps her head down and nods. "It's fine. I should've been watching where I was going." She goes to sidestep him, but he reaches a hand out to stop her.

"Taylor, right?"

She blinks up at him, taking in the floppy chestnut hair and warm smile.

"Oh, um." She steps back, taking stock of her attire and for once regretting the choice to wear pyjamas. "Yeah, yes." She swallows.

"Brodie... from the library?" He hooks a thumb over his shoulder towards town.

"Yeah, I know." She raises her hand in an awkward wave then curtsies for reasons she can't quite fathom. "Heeey."

He chuckles, raking a hand through his hair. "You live around here too?"

She stares at him, assessing what his intentions are. *You have to learn to trust people again.*

"Uh, yeah, I do." She nods her head in the vague direction of home, rocking back on her heels. "So..." She looks around for something else to say. "You come here often then?" She opens her eyes wide and immediately wants to kick herself for sounding like she's pulling a line on him. "I don't mean *here* like I'm hitting on you, but like *here*... at this fish and chip shop... because you like to eat fish and chips too? Ugh, I mean, like you live around here too?" *Oh Good Lord.* She can't stop her mouth from speaking. How has she made a job out of words when she can't even find them in the moment?

Brodie grins. "Yeah, I moved into Porter Street about a month ago, and yes, I'm also ashamed to say I've frequented this place a shocking number of times since then." He grimaces. "Downfall of living on my own, I guess. No one to hold me accountable."

Taylor finds herself smiling. "Yeah, I know what you mean. I kind of forgot to do the groceries, so it was either this or sour milk and cheese." She scrunches her nose up, and he laughs, deep and throaty. The sound does something to her insides, something she hasn't felt in a long time. Warmth, and a kind of fullness of the chest. It makes her want to say something else to make him laugh, just so she can hear it again.

"I don't suppose you want to join me?" He holds his parcel up. "We could sit at one of the tables out front?"

"Oh, I don't know." Her teeth worry at her lower lip. Is he asking her on a date?

"Honestly, I overordered, and you'd be doing me a huge favour by eating with me." He grins. "My waistline already has beef with me."

Taylor can't help but lower her gaze to his midsection, where she can see not an ounce of fat. He's either been graced with great genes, or he works out. Either way, there's no way his feed of fish and chips is going to be detrimental to his physique. Still, that's no reason to say no to the guy. Lynette seems to think he's alright, so maybe it's time to listen to her.

"Sure. Okay, that would be nice. Thanks." She spins on her heels, and he places his hand to the small of her back, guiding her to the tables outside. A tiny flutter of butterflies takes flight in her stomach at the simple gesture. Apparently she's that touch deprived that an innocent placement of hand is enough to render her speechless.

"Here." He pulls a seat out for her, and she lowers herself into it.

"Thanks."

He places the parcel on the table then taps a finger to his chin. "One second." He darts back inside, and she watches as he points to the shelf behind the counter. When he comes back, he's carrying a small tin of tomato sauce and two cans of lemonade. "Can't have fish and chips without sauce. I believe that's sacrilege in some places."

She holds back a snort, but nods. "Oh yes, I've heard that too."

"We can't upset the takeaway gods."

"Oh no, and definitely not when we're about to enjoy their bounty."

"My thoughts exactly." He pulls the ring on top of the can and eases it open then places it on the table between them. "I hope you're hungry." His fingers deftly work at unwrapping the parcel until he has it spread open across the table. "I ordered enough to feed a small army, so take your pick." He gestures to the pile of food. "Ladies first."

Taylor peers down at the steaming goodness, and her stomach lets out an anticipatory grumble. She counts a hotdog, sausage, fish, chicken nuggets, two different donuts, and a mountain of chips. Her eyebrows rise. "You were going to eat this all by yourself?"

His cheeks redden as he offers her his hand. "Hi, I'm Brodie, and I panic when I get flustered." He shrugs.

"There was a queue of people behind me and too many options to choose between."

She stifles a laugh behind her hand. "So you ordered one of everything?"

He rubs a hand down his face, laughing. "It looks that way, doesn't it?" He shakes his head. "A little pressure, and I cave. I would be the ultimate consumer if I was ever put in a high stakes' shopping environment."

She nods. "I get it. There's nothing more high stakes than people waiting in line for food. You're literally in between them and sustenance." She shudders. "It's the thing of nightmares, that is."

"You jest, but it's a serious problem. I have no self-control. However, if you've ever got to fill your grocery trolley before the store closes in ten minutes, I'm your guy." He points both thumbs back at himself. "You won't even know what half of the food items are, but you won't go hungry."

"Wow, that's some superpower."

"It is. And one I take seriously. No one will cram as much unnecessary stuff into their purchase as me, you can be sure of that."

"Your parents must be so proud."

"Oh they are. Every person they meet has to hear the story of my heroics." He rolls his eyes. "It's exhausting, but what can you do?"

"I can't even believe I'm sitting here with *the* Brodie, the man singlehandedly responsible for keeping the economy running. No one will believe me when I tell them." She gives him a bemused smile.

"And what about you? Any superpowers you're hiding?" He tears a piece of fish in half and takes a bite.

"Nothing quite as impressive as yours I'm afraid. But I *can* and *will* leap over a small child if I see a spider coming towards me."

"Mmhmm, mmhmm." He nods knowingly. "Now is that *all* spiders, or just the big ones?"

"Oh, I'm not… arachnist? My fear does not discriminate."

"So one of those quick-moving house spiders with the red legs?"

"You won't see me for dust."

"Interesting."

"Those suckers move far too fast for my liking. It's unnatural."

"Mmm, they are particularly quick wee blighters, I'll give you that." He taps his chin. "What about daddy long legs? Poisonous, yes, but harmless to us humans."

A shudder runs down her spine. "They are even worse. Especially when you're in the shower and they start spelunking down the wall. What are you meant to do then? You're all wet, so you can't run, and you certainly can't turn your back on it."

"I see the dilemma."

"You end up in a stare down with the thing, until one of you, hopefully the spider, ends up down the drain."

"That *is* the best possible scenario for all concerned."

Toying with the tab on the can of lemonade, she nods.

He dusts his hands off. "Let's make a pact."

"I'm listening." She leans forward.

"Next time there's a spider you need dealt with, I'll be your wing man, and vice versa when I'm in a panic-buying situation. Deal?"

Taylor can't help but grin at him. "Deal."

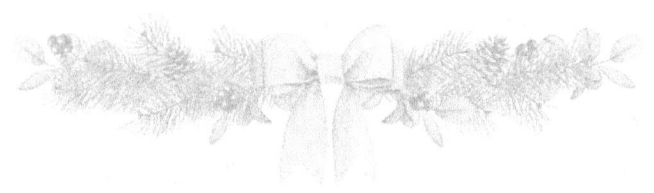

Chapter five

"It's November. Time is ticking away. How's that book coming along? Almost ready for me?" Pam's nasally voice whines through the speaker.

Taylor glances towards the wordcount at the bottom of her screen. 12,754 words. Still not a complete novel, and definitely not as far along as she should be by now. "It's getting there. Just a few tweaks here and there." She grimaces at the lie. For someone who spends their life making up stories about people, she finds it extremely difficult to diverge from the truth in real life.

"Good, good. So, we're still on track for December then? I need to get the editor booked and work on our marketing strategy. Have you got an updated blurb for me?"

"Ah, yes, I'll make sure you have it on time, no worries there. I need a few more days on the blurb. You know how it is, characters changing the story on me." She forces a laugh.

"So I've heard. Makes no sense to me, but that's why you're the writer and I'm the agent. Have it to me by Friday so I can get the cover design in progress."

Friday? That's two days from now. "Sure thing, Pam." Nausea swirls in the pit of her stomach. "I'll get onto that straight away."

"Excellent. We want to keep up that momentum. Strike while the going is good, or whatever it is they say." There's a sound of shuffling papers, then a cough. "Right. I have a Zoom in fifteen, so I'll leave you to it. I'll be waiting for your email."

"Yup," Taylor starts before realising Pam has already clicked off the call. "Shit, shit, shit. What am I going to do, Atticus? I have two days to finalise my blurb, and I haven't even finished the first draft yet." She buries her nose in Atticus's fluff, letting the hum of his purr lull her into a relaxed state. "Thanks, buddy. You always know what I need." Giving him a scratch under the chin, she turns her attention back to the computer and notebooks strewn across the desk. She has one for each book in the series, and each one has crucial information she needs to remember, like timelines and injuries, who lives where and with whom. The oldest notebook, from the first novel she wrote, has loose pages hanging out from where she'd attempted to plot until she realised her characters had a mind of their own and would do whatever they wanted. Plan be damned. From then onwards, Taylor sat at the computer and let her fingers do the walking. Most of the time she was just as surprised as her readers at what was going to come out. And she found she actually preferred it that way. A bit of mystery to keep her on her toes, never knowing exactly where each story will take her, who will survive and who won't.

The only problem with that writing style, is that a blurb doesn't come so easily until the book is near completion. After all, if she doesn't know what's going to happen, how is she meant to write something to entice a reader to pick the book up?

Rummaging back through her scrawled notes, she finds a rough plot idea and fine-tunes a few points until she has the semblance of an outline. A plotter she isn't, but a pantser she cannot afford to be this late in the game. With a two-day deadline for the blurb, she's going to have to pull finger and wrangle her characters into toeing the line, or face the wrath of Pam, and, quite frankly, the characters are easier to control.

Once she finalises the blurb, she has two weeks, at most, to come up with another thirty thousand words to complete the book. Not an easy task, but not undoable either.

Especially when she's already much further along than she had been a week ago before Lynette and her scheme to lure her back out into the world. And really, it hadn't been all that bad, if you set aside the part where she told them all Taylor's secret, the rest had been rather pleasant. She'd laughed for the first time in a long time, and she'd felt that spark of life again. She hadn't realised how much she'd missed that. Perhaps the reclusive life isn't as much her bag as she'd thought it was. Maybe she could learn to trust this group Lynette speaks so highly of. It would be nice to have others to talk to once in a while. Some days the only conversations she has are with herself or Atticus, and he isn't much of a conversationalist.

She can try to let them in to a small portion of her life, but letting them know her nom-de-plume, however, is a whole other kettle of fish. She isn't quite ready to let them in on that one, and quite frankly, she isn't sure she ever will be. Aside from Lynette and Pam, no one else knows. As far as her family is concerned, she puts her degree to use as a freelance editor, which isn't entirely untrue. She did start out in that profession, editing for other authors who were starting out in the business, and she still does the occasional one here and there. She'd probably be doing it full time if Pam hadn't taken her under her wing and kept her going after the Jeremy debacle.

She'd fallen for his wit and charm, and he'd treated her like a queen… until he discovered she'd been writing a novel and had interest from agents. He'd shown his true colours then, and she'd found out exactly what he was capable of when he had dollar signs in his eyes. Poor judge of character, that's what she'd chalked it up to, and she'd made damn sure it wouldn't happen again.

She pushed everyone away except for Lynette, Pam, and her family. She no longer trusted herself to choose the right people to surround herself with, so she just stopped being around people altogether.

For two years that was her life; days spent in solitude, tucked away in her office with her computer and bucket loads of coffee.

Two years of her life keeping herself to herself because she was too afraid to let anyone else in. So maybe it is time to change things up.

Chapter six

"Knock knock!" Lynette lets herself in as she knocks. "I bring coffee and donuts." She holds up two takeaway cups and a brown paper bag. "Coconut vanilla latte for you and a triple shot cappuccino for me." She slides one across the counter towards Taylor then tears into the bag. "Chocolate or caramel?"

Taylor pulls open a drawer and hands her a knife. "Both."

"I like your thinking." She lines up each one and slices through the centre with surgeon-like precision before taking a large bite out of one.

"To what do I owe the pleasure?" Taylor asks, nabbing a piece of each and placing them on a paper towel. "Not that I'm complaining or anything. You just don't normally bring me sweet treats."

Lynette places a hand to her chest as if scandalised. "Are you suggesting that I'm trying to butter you up?"

"I mean, if the shoe fits." Taylor shrugs, tugging the lid off her drink and inhaling the sweet aroma.

"I resent that. I don't *only* bring you the goods when I want something from you."

Taylor gives her a side-eye. "Mmhmm."

"I don't!"

"Okay, okay. Easy, Tiger." Taylor chuckles. "I was only joking around."

"I should hope so. I am nothing if not giving." She peels the lid back on her drink and dunks the chocolate donut into her coffee then quickly brings it to her mouth before it disintegrates.

Taylor screws her nose up. "What on earth compelled you to do that?"

Slurping up the coffee dribbling down her chin, she tilts her head back to speak around the soggy mess. "Saw it on TikTok. Thought I'd give it a go."

"Did you not learn from the cloud bread?" Taylor shakes her head. The last time Lynette tried a TikTok trend was when she attempted to make cloud bread, which left a horrendous doughy smell through the house, and it just looked like a giant, weirdly coloured blob on the tray. Sadly, the taste wasn't good enough to redeem it either.

"Okay, but this is coffee and donuts, the perfect marriage. You should try it. It's actually pretty good."

"I think I'll pass. The texture alone is not appealing in the slightest. Soggy bread is not my thing."

"Uh, what do you think happens when bread is in your mouth, Tay? It gets soggy." She raises her eyebrows, her chin jutting out in her what's-wrong-with-you stance.

"Two very different things. But you do you. I'll just have my coffee in one hand and my donut in the other, and never the twain shall meet."

Lynette rolls her eyes. "You're such a nerd sometimes."

"A nerd who makes money out of said nerdiness."

"Touche."

Taylor grins, leaning down, her elbows on the counter, and her chin in her hands. "I wasn't going to tell you this, because I know how you're going to react, but I'm actually too happy about it to care."

"Ooh, I'm listening." Lynette mimics her stance, resting her own chin in her hands.

"Well, you saw the pitiful wordcount I had last week." Lynette nods. "I might have found some inspiration since then." She pulls her lips in, running her tongue along the crease before releasing her breath. "As of half an hour ago, I'm at 20k."

"Holy shit, Tay, that's awesome! I'm so proud of you."

"Thanks."

"So you'll make the deadline?"

"I think I might, yeah." She nods, a content smile on her face.

"And you weren't going to tell me because?" She quirks a brow.

Taylor sighs. "Because…"

Lynette suddenly leaps up, flinging her hands into the air. "Oh my god, I know why. Because I made you go out, right? That's what inspired you and you didn't want an I-told-you-so moment."

Taylor winces. "I mean, maybe?"

"Well the joke's on you because I'm not going to say a thing." She pretends to zip up her lips. "I might think it," she says under her breath, "but I won't say it."

"You just did."

"What? No I never." Again, she feigns offense, as if Taylor doesn't know her every trick.

"It's fine. You can say it. You were right." She says it in a tone that suggests it pains her to do so. "Ugh. I think I just threw up a little in my mouth."

"You know what? I'm going to take the high road and not even gloat a little bit that my actions led to you completing the unfinishable."

"It wasn't—"

Lynette stops her with a finger in the air. "Uh-uh-uh. Don't rain on my parade. You said I was right, no takebacks."

"Fine." Taylor chuckles. "I'll let you have it. You were right to make me go out."

"I knew it!"

"Don't go getting too cocky."

"I wouldn't dream of it." She dunks another piece of donut into her coffee. "But I *am* pleased to hear it, because I have something different for us to do today."

Taylor's stomach clenches. "We're not going to the library?"

"Oh no, we are. Just not for book club this time." Lynette gives her an appraising look. "What's going on here?" She waggles a finger up and down in Taylor's direction. "Why are you being weird?"

Taylor shakes her head, scrumpling up her used paper towel and dabbing at the corners of her mouth before tossing it into the bin. "I'm not being weird."

"Yes, you are." Lynette squints her eyes. "You looked worried when I said we were doing something different."

"Nope. Not worried." She continues tidying the bench.

Lynette folds her arms. "Uh-huh."

"Uh-huh what?"

"Uh-huh, I think I know what it is." A sly grin stretches across her face. "You actually like it there, don't you?"

"I didn't say that."

"Well, if it's not the library itself, then it's some*one* at the library."

Taylor's cheeks flush, and she turns her back, padding towards the hall. "I'll just grab my shoes then we can go."

"Hoo hoo!" Lynette sings, clapping her hands. "I'm right, aren't I?"

"I don't know what you're talking about," she calls from down the hall.

"Yes you do. That's two for two." She brushes her hand across her shoulder. "I *knew* you'd like him."

Taylor pokes her head around the doorframe. "Again, I didn't say that."

"You didn't have to. Your face said it for you. You're gonna have to work on that poker face if you wanna try and pull one over on me. You know I can read you like a book." She dances towards her best friend, singing, "You like Brodie."

She looks so absurd, Taylor can't help but laugh. "You're such a dork."

"A dork who is the queen of matchmakers though."

"Need I remind you of judo jumper guy again?"

"Shh, let's not focus on the negatives, and instead focus on what you're going to wear on your first date!"

"Whoa there, Nelly. No one said anything about a date." Not that she would be averse to getting to know him a little better. After all, she *had* found him good to talk to the other night. But dating? No.

"Maybe not right now, but it will happen. I can feel it in my bones." She wiggles her fingers in the air. "You two were made for each other."

Chapter seven

"Art class?" Taylor gives her friend a sceptical look. "I know I'm a creative writer, but that's the extent of creative bones in my body. I can't even draw a stick man."

Lynette snorts. "Trust me. I didn't think I was any good either until I came to one of these." She inhales deeply, her eyes closed, and her hands swirling circles in front of her, as if summoning good things. "Enjoy the process."

"Lynette, Taylor. Lovely to see you both. Come, come." Brodie ushers them into a well-lit room. There are three large tables covered with drop cloths, and sheets of glass at each station.

"Are we doing some sort of stained-glass painting?" Taylor asks in a whisper.

"Uh, no. Those are for mixing paint."

"Oh, right."

"Take a seat, everyone, and we'll get started." Brodie waits until all eyes are on him before speaking again. "With Christmas looming, I thought we could do some artworks that could be given as gifts or used to decorate the home." He smiles, reaching for a sheet of paper. "I have some ideas here, which I'll hand out. Now, these are for inspiration, so don't feel like you have to do what's here. Think of a theme, like family or love, and let your mind wander." He walks around distributing the worksheets. "I have three different canvas sizes for you to choose from. Small squares, slightly larger rectangles, or these ones with the arch at the top."

"I think I'll just go with the small one please," Taylor says as he approaches. "I've not really done much on the art front before."

"Hey, that's what this is all about though. A place to express yourself and try something new." He hands her a canvas. "What about you, Lynette?"

"The arch please."

Once all the canvases have been handed out, he selects one for himself. "Now, I like to start by giving my canvas a base coat. It can be whatever colour you want it to be. One colour, two, a gradient. It's entirely up to you. Just add a little water to thin it out and then glide your brush across the canvas like so." He demonstrates with a pastel blue colour. "You should be able to find most colours in the boxes on your tables, but if there's anything you can't find, sing out, and I'll see if I can find you one."

Light chatter and laughter fills the room as everyone gets to work laying their base coats down. Taylor stares blankly at her canvas. "I don't even know where to start."

"That's okay. Do you perhaps have a favourite colour? Or is there an image on the sheet that you'd like to try recreating?" Brodie suggests, crouching beside her.

Her pulse quickens. "I do like the look of this one." She points to a more abstract-looking image. "I don't think I could do any of the others. I can't draw people." She laughs under her breath.

"Okay, see how this one has a lot of greens and blues in it? You could choose one or both for your base.

59

You're going to be layering over it, so whatever you choose, it won't hinder your final piece."

She glances at Lynette who has already filled half her canvas with a golden yellow. Letting out a soft sigh, she selects a brush and a tube of turquoise paint.

"Try this one instead." Brodie holds out a thicker brush. "It's a bit softer and will give a smoother base for you to start with." As he moves towards the next table, he pats her shoulder gently. The touch sends a shiver down her spine, but in a good way.

Dipping her brush into the water then dabbing it at the blob of turquoise paint on her glass plate, she inhales deeply before swiping it across her canvas. It goes on thick in parts and watery in others, but she slowly gets the hang of it, blending the colours across until the canvas is coated. Everyone is lined up to use the hairdryer before moving onto the next step, so she follows suit, feeling out of her depth. It seems as though she's the only one there who doesn't know what they're doing.

Once her paint is dry, she sits back down and notices that everyone else is just getting on with it. Lynette has outlined a pier with a couple sitting at the end and a dog between them. The upper portion of her canvas is golden yellow, and the lower half is a mix of blues and greens, and it's already beginning to take shape.

"Is that your parents?" Taylor asks, pointing at the couple.

"Yeah, with Dusty." Lynette grins. "Thought I might give it to them for Christmas if it turns out okay."

"Are you kidding? It's already amazing. I had no idea you could do this." Taylor watches her friend's hand move deftly across the canvas. It's a side to her she's never seen before.

Lynette laughs. "I'm nothing special. It's just a bit of fun and a creative outlet, I guess. Like writing is for you." She nudges her with her elbow. "You should see what some of the others do though. They're inspiring."

"*You're* inspiring, Lynny. You have it all figured out, and I don't even know where to begin."

Brodie swoops down from behind her. "How're we going here, ladies?"

"Great," Lynette says.

"Umm." Taylor looks pensive. "I don't really know what to do next."

Brodie chuckles. "We all have to start somewhere, right?" He reaches over the table and grabs a piece of charcoal. "Here, outline what you want the image to be."

She chews her lip. "Okay…" She lets the word draw out as she scrapes the charcoal into two lopsided arches to form somewhat of a heart. "Like that?"

"Exactly. Now you just add colour to make it pop. You can use the brushes like Lynette is, or you could try dabbing with a sponge or some scrumpled up paper to give a more rustic look." He points across the table. "See what Jenny is doing with the sponge? Why don't you give that a try?"

She nods, still not feeling overly confident. Starting with more of the turquoise, she dabs the sponge across the top corner then slowly adds blues and purples until the heart is surrounded by colour. Then she selects a thin brush and paints a black outline around the heart, then goes back over it with her sponge to smudge it in.

"That looks great," Brodie says as he passes by. "Now you just need to add in some lighter colours to bring it to the foreground and give it dimension." He points to the sample image she's using as a template. "See how they've used a pale pink here and a darker red here?"

After twenty minutes of dabbing, she leans back, giving her creation an appraising eye. "It needs something else."

Lynette leans over. "That looks great, Tay."

"Mmm, I don't know."

"Oh, why don't you try adding some wee hearts? Brodie has a few stencils. You could try adding some bright red ones down one side, maybe a few lighter ones near the top of the canvas too?"

Taylor glances towards her friend's masterpiece and figures she must know what she's talking about. Give her a blank sheet of paper and a typewriter, and she can create something beautiful, but ask her to create a picture from her own mind, and she draws a blank. The artistic gene skipped her when it was handed out.

"Brodie, where are those stencils you have?" Lynette calls out.

"Oh, right here." He pulls an elasticated bundle from one of the paint boxes.

"Taylor wants to add some hearts."

"Good choice." He smiles, sauntering over and crouching beside her. "All you do is place it where you want it, then again, using your brush or sponge, colour in the ones you want to use."

"Thanks." Her fingers brush against his as she takes it from him, and her cheeks warm. "Um, like this?" She positions it over the right side of the heart.

"If that's where you want them to go."

Turning her focus to the job at hand, she dabs a vibrant red into the holes, then lifts the stencil and places it further down to give it an elongated look.

"That looks great." He pats her shoulder, and she can't help but smile broadly up at him, then silently admonishes herself for it. She has to keep reminding herself that he's just a nice guy, and she's not looking to get involved. Unfortunately, her face and her heart don't seem to have received the memo.

"Right," Brodie addresses the room. "I'd love to give you all afternoon to finish up, but the library does close in an hour, so we'll need to be mindful of that. Let's give it another fifteen minutes, then we'll need to start packing up." He moves around the tables, pointing out what he likes and offering suggestions to help bring more out in each piece of art. He's patient and attentive, making sure he gets around to everyone.

Taylor tidies up a few hearts that went astray, then holds her painting out at arm's length. "What do you think?"

Lynette glances up from her work. "Yup, the hearts really finished it. Nice work." She winks, tossing her hair back. "I knew you'd be into this." Her eyes dart towards

Brodie, and a grin tugs at her lips as she turns her attention back to her artwork. Taylor chooses to ignore her not-so-subtle hint.

"Yeah, you know, this painting gig isn't half bad. There's something freeing about it."

"I feel the same way," Brodie says, looking over her shoulder. "No matter what kind of day you're having, once you pick up a paintbrush or a sponge and start flinging paint at a canvas, everything melts away." He waves his hand through the air as if following a current.

Lynette quirks a brow. "I mean, yeah, but for me it's that I can bugger it up and it doesn't matter because I can just paint over it and start again. That's pretty freeing."

Brodie laughs. "Yes, there is that too."

"I suppose it's kind of like writing in that respect. Delete or backspace and start again." Taylor nods to herself.

"Creativity is a beautiful thing," Brodie adds, "There's no right or wrong." He points down at Taylor's canvas. "Well done with this. I hope we see you back here again." He begins gathering up loose tubes of paint and popping them back in the tub.

"You know, I think you might."

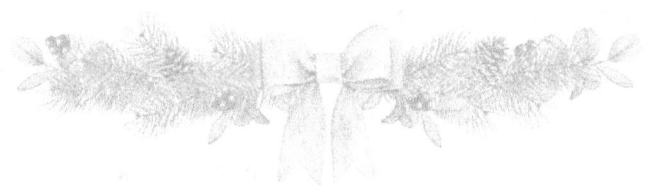

Chapter eight

"And send." Taylor closes her eyes and clicks the button before she can change her mind. "Blurb complete. Now to finish the rest of the book and make it work." She grimaces at Atticus, who has sprawled himself across her notebooks.

Shooing him out of the way, she picks one up and writes in the blurb to keep her on track, then flicks through the tabs to find what she needs for the next scene where the heroine goes foraging for the first time.

She sets a timer on her phone and pushes it to the far end of her desk, so it doesn't distract her, then puts in her earbuds and zones in on the screen in front of her.

The book has been coming along much faster since she's allowed herself to venture out into the world again, and she can see a light at the end of the tunnel. She *will* make her deadline.

A song by the Broods plays while she delves back into her novel's world and creates a woodland for her FMC to traverse. She barely refers to her carefully planned notes, allowing the story to flow from her fingertips until a glance at the corner of the screen says she's been at it for nearly three hours. In that time, she's managed to write another eight thousand words, and the climax of the story is approaching.

She pulls her earbuds out and jolts at the sudden pain in her neck. Perhaps three hours is a little too long to be so intensely focused on a screen. She twists her neck side-to-side, then up and down, all while pressing her fingertips into the flesh to relieve some of the built-up tension.

Atticus hasn't returned since she shooed him away, which is unusual for him. Even when he's had a telling off, he still likes to hover and make his presence known. Frowning, Taylor pushes her seat back and peers beneath the desk. No sign of him there. She pads down the hall towards the kitchen, coming to an abrupt stop when she sees the kitchen window wide open.

"Oh no. No, no, no, no, no." She rushes over and looks outside to see an envelope and nothing else. "Atticus!" she calls, dashing through every room in the house. "Atticus, here boy!" Tears prick her eyes as she replays the afternoon over in her mind. She'd come in from checking the mail and been surprised by a spider that crawled out from between two envelopes. She'd had no qualms in opening the window and depositing the spider, envelope and all, outside, then proceeded to scrub at her hands until she could no longer feel the thousands of creepy crawly legs she was sure were all over her. For the life of her, though, she cannot recall if she'd closed the window or not.

Atticus is an indoors cat. He is also as spoilt as they come. He has his own room with a large cat tree in one corner, an oversized fluffy pillow to sleep on in another corner, and one of those enclosed litter boxes for added privacy. At this point, he's practically a flatmate. But he *never* goes outside.

Never.

Slipping on a pair of jandals, Taylor heads for the door, all the while calling his name. She does a full circuit of the house then stops at the edge of the drive. A lump forms in her throat as she works up the courage to go onto the street and look.

"Taylor? Is everything okay?" a familiar voice says, and a fresh wave of tears cascade down her cheeks. "Oh my God, what's happened?" Brodie gathers her hands in his. "You're shaking."

"I… it's…" she hiccups. "It's Atticus. He's gone."

"Atticus?"

"M-my c-cat."

He glances over his shoulder. "Gone?"

She nods. "I must've left the window open. He's never been outside before. He doesn't know his way around or to look for cars."

"Well what does he look like? I'll help you look for him, okay? I'm sure he's just hiding out somewhere safe."

She nods again. "I hope so." Her voice is barely a whisper. "He's grey but with tabby markings and bright blue eyes. He's shorter than a lot of other cats, and a little bit chunky."

"Okay, you stay here, and I'll go and check the roadside, just to be sure." He gives her hands a squeeze then moves to the curb. He peers down both sides before returning. "All clear. Do you have a picture of him? Maybe we could go door-to-door."

Taylor pulls out her phone. "I have heaps." She scrolls to find one that shows his face and markings clearly.

"He's adorable." Brodie smiles. "Okay, let's try the houses either side of you first. He won't have ventured far for his first time out in the wild."

It strikes her that he could so easily be describing her. Two outings, three if you include the fish and chip night, and neither one far from her home.

They walk up the narrow path of the house next door, sidestepping the overgrown shrubbery and several yellow diggers strewn about the place. Brodie knocks and steps back, his arm brushing against Taylor's, offering some comfort. She's lived next door for two years and managed to avoid both neighbours. Such is the reclusive lifestyle.

The door creaks open and a young woman with her hair tied in a messy bun atop her head peeks her head around the edge. "Can I help you?" She eyes first Taylor, then Brodie.

"Hopefully." He looks to Taylor, who has clammed up. "Have you seen a cat hanging around this afternoon?

A grey one?" He gestures to Taylor, and she hands her phone to the woman as she steps outside.

"He's really friendly and loves to cuddle."

The woman stares at the phone for a beat. "Sorry, no. But we have a tomcat here who can get quite territorial, so I doubt he would've let another cat come close." She hands the phone back to Taylor.

"Okay." Brodie nods. "Thank you anyway." He waves, and they turn back towards the street. "Let's try your other neighbour. Maybe we'll have better luck there."

Taylor follows, her eyes downcast as she scans the bushes and fencelines nearby. She's so focused she doesn't notice Brodie stop in front of her.

"Oof." She stumbles backwards, her heel catching on the edge of the footpath.

"Oh shit, sorry." He grasps her hand, catching her before she falls into the gutter, but not before her ankle twists at an odd angle. "Are you okay?"

She shakes her head, brushing herself off. "I'm fine. Sorry, wasn't watching where I was going."

"No, no, it was my fault. I thought I heard something and just stopped right in front of you." He presses his finger and thumb to his temple. "Are you sure you're okay? It looked like you caught your ankle."

Standing on one foot, she gives the other a tentative swivel, sucking a breath through her teeth.

Brodie's chin dips. "I knew it. God, Taylor I'm so sorry. Here I am trying to help you, and I make it ten times worse."

"It's fine. I think I just tweaked it."

"Here." He wraps an arm around her waist and takes the brunt of her weight. "Let me help you get back inside so you can get some ice on it, and then I'll come back out and keep up the search."

"I can't ask you to do that."

"Please, it's the least I can do." He guides her back up her drive and waits while she unlocks the door then helps her into the kitchen. Once inside, he sets her down on a dining chair then drags another one in front for her foot. He adds a cushion and ever so gently lifts her foot and places it on top before going to the freezer for ice.

A moment later he returns with a tea towel parcel of ice and lowers it onto her ankle. "Here, keep this on it. I'll do a quick zip around the neighbourhood."

"You really don't have to—"

He holds up a hand, palm out. "I know I don't. But we can't have Atticus wandering around aimlessly now, can we?" He pushes himself up to standing. "I won't be long. Like I said, he won't have gone far."

Chapter nine

"If I were a cat, where would I go?" Brodie stands on the porch, looking across the yard. Dense shrubbery adorns the front fence line and along the side of the drive, which would make for a good hiding spot, but surely Atticus would've come running if he'd heard his name being called.

Stepping off the porch, he drops to his knees and peers into the small grate cut into the concrete foundation. "Atticus," he calls, adding a few clicks of the tongue for reasons unknown to him. He's never had a cat of his own before, but for some reason, it seems the right noise to make.

After a few more calls and no answer or sounds of movement, he climbs back to his feet and edges around to the side of the property. There's a tall, locked gate, that he unlatches and swings open, careful to shut it behind him. This side of the house is even more overgrown than the front. Either Taylor isn't much of a gardener, or she's trying to discourage people from entering.

He passes the open kitchen window and makes a beeline for the garden shed down the back of the property. If there was ever a place to hide out, that would be it. The corrugated iron sheeting has seen better days; holes and rust spots wend their way around the corners and front of the shed. The wooden door hangs unevenly from its hinges and is slightly ajar. He gives the bottom a nudge with his foot. "Atticus?"

Nothing.

With one hand lifting the door so it doesn't drag along the dirt, he pulls it all the way open, stepping inside. "Atticus?" The space is small with little in it bar a shovel and a rusty push mower leaned up against the work top. Aside from spiders hanging out in the corner of the room and window ledge, there's not a living soul inside.

He's about to step outside when he hears a soft mewling sound from somewhere behind him. Spinning on his heels, he scans the shed interior again, slower this time. "Atticus?"

There it is again, only it's not from inside the shed, but outside. Brodie makes his way back outside, closing the door behind him. "Atticus?" he calls again, and this time the response is a little louder and coming from up high. Tucked in behind the shed is a tall cabbage tree, but there's no sign of Atticus there. Thank God. He wants to help Taylor out, but shimmying up a cabbage tree, or anything really, is not something he fancies doing.

Brodie cranes his neck up at the large oak at the opposite end of the garden. There, tucked between two knotted branches near the trunk and about halfway up, sits a grey ball of fluff.

"Atticus?" he tries again, and the cat meows back at him. "Of course." He sighs. Tree climbing was never his forte as a child. He was more of an arts and crafts kid or a hide-and-seek in the library kid.

Scratching his head, he tosses up his choices. There was no sign of a ladder in the shed, and he hadn't spied one on the periphery of the garden either, which means he's either going to have to go old school and use his arms and legs, or he's going to have to call someone in to help.

He looks back towards the house. Taylor had been beside herself, if he calls the fire brigade to come and rescue Atticus, she'll panic. No, he can't do that to her. There's only one thing for it.

He pulls his sleeves up and marches towards the towering behemoth. It can't be that hard, kids do it all the time. Finding a small knot at waist height, he hoists one leg up, resting his toes on the lip. Above, there are several thick branches just out of reach. With a deep inhale, he shifts his weight to the foot on the tree and pushes up from the ground, only to land back where he was. Not enough oomph.

Taking another breath, he tries again, this time wrapping his arms around the trunk of the tree, effectively hugging it rather than scaling the thing. Still, he can't give up now. His free leg dangles limply, so he slings it around the trunk like a child on their parent's leg.

"Okay." He grunts, his face pressed against the rough bark. "I can do this." Inch by inch, he straddles his way up the trunk until his fingers can grasp the closest branch. A light sheen of sweat covers his brow already as he manages to lob himself up enough that his elbow now holds him in place with the branch.

Atticus meows from several metres above as he watches the slow progress of his rescuer.

"You could help me out, buddy."

Atticus swishes his tail, meowing again.

"I'm trying."

Brodie drags his foot up the trunk until he finds another knot, this one a little bigger. Finding purchase, he catapults himself upward, wrapping both arms around the branch, both legs swinging out from under him.

He turns his gaze skyward. "You couldn't have found something lower to the ground to get stuck in? There's a perfectly good shed over there that would've made my life a whole lot easier."

He hoists one leg over then the other, then comes to a seated position, catching his breath. There are at least another five branches to climb, and already he's regretting his decision.

The next three branches aren't quite as difficult as the first, and he shimmies up there with ease. The fourth, however, is a long way up, and there doesn't appear to be any knots or smaller branches he can use to help.

"Atticus? Come on, boy. Jump down to me. It's not that far," he calls up, knowing it's likely futile. The cat hasn't strayed from its spot other than to clean himself or swat at bugs flying past. Still, it was worth a shot to save himself the agony of climbing yet another bough.

Shuffling in close to the trunk, he wraps both arms around it and slowly edges himself up to stand atop the branch. He doesn't dare look down.

His fingers crawl up over the bark, searching for a holding spot, but as he first thought, there are none. He huffs out a sigh, closing his eyes. Now what?

Craning his neck, he assesses the distance to the next branch. Now that he's standing, it doesn't appear as high as he thought. Maybe a foot above where his hands can reach. He takes a tentative step out from the trunk and balances himself. Swallowing the lump in his throat, he exhales through his mouth then sucks air in through his nose and leaps.

Chapter ten

One hand grasps the branch, and his heart thunders in his chest as his body swings aimlessly below. Physical strength is not Brodie's strong suit. He prefers to hone his finer motor skills in the arts and creative ventures. Climbing trees, rough and tumble; all that physical stuff has never interested him. Completely out of his wheelhouse now, Brodie tries desperately to swing his body up enough that his arm or leg, or both, can grab hold.

Like a child on the monkey bars, he rocks back, extending his arm as far as possible, then launches forward. His free hand grabs hold and he uses the forward momentum to swing a leg over. Out of breath, and sweating profusely, he clings on for dear life, squinching his eyes closed. Heights have never bothered him before, but then again, he's never been daft enough to climb a tree this high before either. Looking down at what could potentially be his final destination doesn't feel like the right thing to do, all things considered.

His pulse races and he can't manage to catch his breath. Though his mind is screaming at him to keep moving, finish the task at hand, his body has other ideas. Frozen to the spot, he can't make even his little toe move. *I guess this is me now*, he thinks, *I'll just live out my days up here.*

A scratching sound from above catches his attention, but not enough to look. Whatever it is, it can come for him. His body has left the building and will no longer cooperate.

Another scratching sound, followed by a meow from Atticus, and suddenly something soft but with pinpricks for feet lands on Brodie's back. The force has his eyes springing open, and all he can see is how far off the ground he is. Black spots dance in front of him.

"No, no, no, no," he mutters, closing his eyes again. Fainting is not on the cards. Not now. He inhales through his nose, holds it for three seconds then lets go with a woosh.

The thing on his back walks in a circle then settles itself between his shoulder blades, a furry tail swishing up to bat around his ears.

Atticus.

The gentle hum of him purring resonates through his chest, which is both soothing and alarming. With Atticus sitting comfortably on his back, he can't comprehend how he'll get them both out of the tree.

He could yell for help, but Taylor is all the way inside with her foot up, and with her sprained ankle, she won't be able to help anyway. There is the neighbour, but she wasn't overly forthcoming, so that seems unlikely too. If he could reach into his back pocket without throwing them off balance, he could call someone, but with Atticus perched where he is and the precarious position he's in, he's not willing to risk it either.

"Well, Atticus, I guess this is it for us," he says, resigned to the fact. "You and I, we live here now." Of all the things he could be doing tonight, getting stuck halfway up a tree with a cat on his back was not how he thought his day would play out.

What feels like hours later, when the sun has shifted behind the clouds, a creak comes from the direction of the house. From his position, he can't see that way, but he can definitely hear the soft sound of footfalls.

"Brodie?" Not the voice he was expecting. "Taylor's getting all antsy that you haven't come back, and she's worried you've fallen down a well or something. You good?"

He clears his throat. "Ah, hey, Lynette." Force of habit has his fingers lifting in somewhat of a wave before he quickly draws them back to the death grip he has on the branch. At this point, both his feet have gone to sleep and the tingling in his arms has been slowly increasing to the point of pain.

"Brodie? Where the hell are you?"

"U-up here." He clears his throat again. "I got a bit stuck."

He can't see her, but he can tell when she spots him because she belts out a laugh so loud it scares Atticus and he digs his claws into Brodie's back.

"Aaaatticus," he hisses beneath his breath, while Lynette clasps her sides, snort-laughing. "It's not *that* funny," he mutters under his breath.

Atticus resettles himself on Brodie's back and begins to clean himself vigorously.

"Do you mind? This is not the place, buddy." He tries to wiggle his back enough that Atticus will stop, but he only clamps down harder with his claws. "Guess I had that coming."

"Say cheese," Lynette says in a sing-song voice from directly below, aiming her phone camera at him. "This is too good."

"You think you could maybe help me?"

She snorts. "And how exactly do you envisage that going down? I know I seem agile, but I'm more orangutan than spider monkey, if you get my drift."

Brodie frowns. "You're covered in hair and have exceptionally long arms?"

She folds her arms across her chest. "I know you're in crisis, so I'm gonna let that one slide. I meant that I can get by on the ground, but me and heights do not go well together."

He closes his eyes. "You do know that orangutans climb trees too, right? In fact, they're quite nimble when it comes to moving about at height. They're kind of opposite to what you just said."

"Man, you really don't want to get out of that tree, do you?" She spins on her heels and starts walking back the way she came.

"No wait!" Again, Atticus digs his claws in, this time accompanied with a hiss. "Please come back."

Lynette sighs like a teenager who's been told to empty the dishwasher. "Fine. I'm still not climbing that tree though. I just had my nails done."

"So, what do we do now then?"

She pulls her phone out again. "I got you, boo."

Chapter eleven

A low rumble comes from the roadside, and Lynette claps her hands. "They're here." She squeals, and all Brodie can hear are her quick footfalls heading away.

"Wait, where are you going?" he cries out. At this point, his arms and legs are set like stone, and he's numb from head to toe. If Atticus sunk his claws in this time, he didn't feel it.

Out front there's a bang and a whoosh, then Lynette's babbling voice coming closer again. The gate creaks open and bangs against the other side.

"This way, boys." Her voice is exuberant, and it has Brodie on edge.

Boys? he thinks.

"See? I told you."

Brodie manages to shift his neck slightly to peer down at the ground. Lynette is there, alongside a burly looking fireman with Taylor in his arms, and two other kitted-out men.

"Atticus!" Taylor cries out. "You found him!"

At the sound of his name, Atticus meows then begins pacing back and forth across Brodie's back, claws and all. At least Taylor looks happy.

"Uh, yeah, I did. Poor fella was stuck up here…" He clears his throat. "And I guess I am now too." A nervous chuckle escapes his lips. This is not at all how he wanted Taylor to see him. Especially not while in the arms of a strapping man who looks like he bench-presses cars daily. *Seriously, how big are those biceps?*

"Don't worry, mate. We'll have you down in no time. Just hang tight," the one with a buzz cut and tattoos down his arms says. He makes his way towards the tree, while the one with red hair and a ZZ Top beard walks off. The guy holding Taylor sets her down on the grass then removes his jersey, balling it up and placing it beneath her foot.

"I'm so sorry, Brodie," she says, peering up at him. "I can't believe you've been stuck up there this whole time."

He pretends to brush it off. "It's nothing. No harm done. I'm just glad I found him."

Red hair comes back with a ladder under his arms. He leans it against the tree trunk, bracing it either side while buzz cut climbs quickly to the top and performs something Brodie's only ever seen done on TV, and it always ended with someone injuring themselves; he swings himself up onto the lower branch then leaps from branch to branch like a parkour expert. He makes it look like a walk in the park, not the death-defying action it really is.

"Alright, mate." He straddles his legs either side of the branch behind Brodie. "I'm here with you. How're you doing? Are you hurt at all?"

"No, I don't think so. I just can't, um, move without seeing black spots and feeling nauseous."

"That's good. We can work with that." He shuffles in. "I'm going to put my hands on your ankles now, okay?"

"Okay."

"I need you to relax and let your feet drop down. You're balanced, and I've got you, so you won't fall. Just let them go." He grabs hold of Brodie's ankles and pulls them apart and away from the branch they've been clinging too for so long. "That's it. Let go. Close your eyes if you need to. I won't let you fall."

He does as he's told, and feels buzz cut shuffle in closer again. His hand lands on his belt, and Brodie flinches. Taylor gasps. "Careful!"

"I'm okay. Sorry."

"Right, I'm going to pull you up towards me, then we're going to climb down, okay? Deep breaths in through the nose and out through the mouth."

Brodie's heart races, but he allows buzz cut to ease him upwards, away from the branch that has been his lifeline for the afternoon.

"You're doing great," Taylor calls up, and he smiles, opening his eyes to see her.

Big mistake.

"Oh—"

"Shit!" Buzz cut wraps his arm around Brodie's waist, catching him before he falls. His body sags, his head slumped against his chest.

"I'm here," the burly one says, balancing at the top of the ladder. "Hand him down to me."

In the weirdest pass the parcel, they pass Brodie's limp body between them until he's safely on the ground.

"Is he okay?" Taylor scuffles closer, placing her hand on his arm.

ZZ Top has his fingers pressed to Brodie's pulse. "He'll be fine. He's still breathing. Might be a little bit of heat stroke or dehydration, depending on how long he's been up there."

Taylor worries her lip. He had been gone a while, and all to find Atticus, who was doing what normal cats do – climbing trees. "God, I feel terrible. This is all my fault."

"You can't blame yourself. And at least you know how he really feels." Buzz cut winks.

Taylor scrunches her nose. "What do you mean? Did he say something?"

He laughs. "Lady, he didn't have to. The guy is obviously terrified of heights, but he still went and climbed a tree to rescue your cat." He holds out his hands, palms up as if weighing something. "Actions, words."

Lynette sidles up to his side, stroking a finger along one of his tattoos. "And what are *my* actions saying?" she purrs.

He clears his throat, removing his arm from her grasp and holding up his ring finger. "They're saying you're trouble."

Lynette pouts, folding her arms across her chest. "Typical. All the good ones are either gay or married."

He chuckles, tipping his head towards the other two. "I have it on good authority that these two are both straight and single." He steps back, gesturing between them. "Have at it."

"Well…" She runs her hand down her front then pushes past him. "Which one of you wants to take me out to celebrate this heroic rescue?"

Chapter twelve

When Brodie comes to, he's lying across an unfamiliar couch with a very familiar lump sitting on his chest. "Hey, buddy." He scratches Atticus behind the ears. "Where am I?" he whispers.

"Oh, you're awake." Taylor hobbles in from the kitchen with two glasses of water. "They said you might be dehydrated, so…" She holds out a glass.

He scoots himself to a sitting position – as much as Atticus will allow him to. "Thanks." He frowns. "Please tell me I didn't really get stuck in a tree and have to be rescued by hunky firemen."

"Oh, you most definitely did." She winces. "I really am sorry about that. I bet you didn't expect to end your day like this."

He shrugs. "Honestly, I've had worse."

Her eyes widen. "Worse than passing out halfway up a giant tree?"

He snorts. "Oh yeah. This is not my first rodeo, unfortunately." He cringes. "I know, it goes against that whole bad boy vibe I've got going on, what with me being a painting librarian and all."

Taylor stifles a laugh. "Just a little bit." She holds her finger and thumb up with barely any space between them.

"Believe it or not, I am not the most coordinated of people."

She eyes his broad shoulders and firm biceps with a quirk of the brow.

He shakes his head. "I like to stay fit, in the hopes that when I do have my oopsie moments, I don't injure myself as much as I used to." He pulls a face. "I had many a broken bone as a child, and all because I was accident prone. I once broke my ankle by bouncing on a trampoline, then sprained the other one two weeks later. That was not a fun summer, I can tell you."

"Oh my." She leans forward. "Would you believe I haven't broken a single bone?"

"Not even your pinkie toe?"

She shakes her head. "Not even that. The closest I came was snapping my front tooth in a game of tag."

He tilts his head. "That's... not what I was expecting. You and I play very different games of tag."

She laughs. "Yeah, I think I'm probably the only person in the world to be able to claim that. I must've been around fifteen; it was in PE at school. We were all running around in the gymnasium and I ran right into the back of this guy's head. Knocked me out cold, and when I came to, I spat my tooth across the floor."

"Wow. I'm impressed. Even I haven't managed to do anything like that, and I've had some doozies." He scrubs his hand down his jaw. "Though, I do feel that counts as a broken bone."

She purses her lips. "Hmmm. Does it though?"

"I mean, is a tooth a bone? No. But am I going to die on this ledge? Absolutely I am." He grins. "Come on. You're already smart, talented, *and* beautiful." Her cheeks flush at the compliment. "You can't be that perfect. There has to be a flaw to you somewhere. It's the law of physics."

"Well, who am I to deny physics?" She brushes an imaginary strand of hair behind her ear.

"Exactly. So, the broken tooth counts." He takes a sip of water then places it on the table. "And on the topic of broken bones, how's your ankle?" He nods towards her bandaged appendage.

"Better. Thanks. Jason wrapped it for me before he left."

"Jason?"

"One of the firemen. The one with the red Gandalf beard."

"Huh. I was thinking it was more like ZZ Top."

Taylor chuckles. "Yeah, I guess I can see that. Anyway—" She glances at her watch. "—he should be clocking off in about fifteen minutes, then he's taking our Lynette out on a date." She grins, bringing her glass to her lips.

"Is that so?" He smiles, shaking his head. "She doesn't waste any time, does she?"

"Nope. Not ever."

"Good on her. I don't think I'm quite that adventurous."

"No?"

"Yeah, no. I'm more of a homebody. Like to keep myself to myself, and I'm much too self-conscious to go out with a complete stranger. That takes guts."

"Oh yeah, she's a go-out-and-get-'em type of girl. If she wants it, she'll make it happen." She splays her hands out at her sides. "Case and point. I never would've come to the library if she hadn't dragged me along."

"Really? But you're a writer. I'd have thought you'd feel right at home there." His eyes bore into hers, as if he's genuinely interested to hear her story.

"Once upon a time, it would've been my favourite place to while away the day. But, you know, things changed. I got burned, and I didn't feel I could trust people anymore." She shrugs. "It was just easier to avoid any kind of social situation."

"I'm sorry you felt that way. The library is meant to be a safe space where everyone is welcome. I'm sorry you felt you couldn't be part of that." He nudges Atticus away, then reaches across and takes her hand. "I hope you feel differently towards it now."

His thumb rubs circles on the back of her hand, and for some reason it makes her want to cry. How can such a simple act have her emotions running riot like this? Why does she find herself wanting to cry at the kindest of gestures? Is this what happens when you deprive yourself of physical touch? God, it's all too much to think about.

"I do." She nods. "It *is* a welcoming place. It's just this voice in the back of my head that won't let me fully relax." She shakes her head. "That probably sounds ridiculous."

"No, not at all." He scoots closer. "I think we all have that voice in our head, we just have to choose whether to listen to it or not."

"Hmm."

"I know it's not the same, but my job is super customer focused, and I love that, but it can be draining sometimes when everyone needs you at once. That's partly why I keep to myself after hours, so I can regroup and be prepared for the next day."

"I can understand that."

"Right? And sometimes it can be hard to convince myself to go in, especially if I know I have a full-on day ahead, but then I stop and remind myself that it's the people that *make* the job what it is. Because of them, I get to work in a place that allows me to explore my creativity and meet people from all walks of life.

"So maybe you need to remind *your*self, and that voice, what's important to you too. What gives you life and fills your cup, you know?"

"You make it sound easy."

He smiles. "Oh, it's not, but it does get easier the more you practise it. Like painting a picture or writing a book; you have to keep at it to hone that skill enough that it becomes second nature. And then, I guess, you won't need to remind yourself anymore." He shrugs.

"I guess I forgot how much I used to like people. As weird as that sounds. I was actually someone who thrived on being around others... until I couldn't anymore."

"It doesn't sound weird. It sounds like you were coping the way you knew how." He brushes a hair behind her ear, tilting her face towards his. "But maybe it's time to try a new strategy."

Her breath catches in her throat as his gaze drops to her lips then back to her eyes. She's torn between wanting him to kiss her and wanting to pull away. Her heart tells her he's nothing like Jeremy, the complete opposite, in fact. And yet, her mind refuses to believe there isn't an ulterior motive.

"Maybe I could try." Her voice comes out in a whisper, her body leaning towards his of its own volition.

He licks his lips. "I think that's a good idea." There's a throaty rasp to his voice. "Taylor?"

"Mmm?"

"Can I kiss you?"

Chapter thirteen

Oh good Lord, yes please. She doesn't trust her voice not to falter, so nods instead, her eyes fluttering closed.

Brodie nuzzles his nose against hers, his palm cupping her jaw. Then ever so gently, his lips brush hers. He pulls back, resting his forehead to hers.

"You okay?" she asks with concern.

"Yeah. I just need a moment."

She places her hands to his chest, his heart thundering rapidly beneath her touch. "Was it that bad?"

He chuckles, closing his eyes and letting his head fall to the crook of her neck. "Far from it."

"Then?"

"I don't want to rush things."

"Brodie." She leans back, taking his face in her hands. "It was a kiss, and barely even that, if I'm honest." His eyes widen, and she grins. "You're gonna have to do better than that, buddy."

He smirks. "Is that so?"

"Oh yeah." She nods. "Do your worst."

"And here I was thinking I should be a gentleman."

She snorts. "What gave you the impression I wanted that?"

He trails a finger languidly down her neck. "It's not that I thought you wanted it, more that I thought you *needed* it." He winces. "Was I wrong?"

"Umm." She sucks in her bottom lip. "I actually don't know."

"Okay?"

"I've never really had that before."

He quirks his brow.

"A nice guy."

"My god, Taylor." He shakes his head, sliding his hand back up to cup around the nape of her neck. "Your bar is way too low."

"The bar hasn't been seen in a long time." She chews her lip. "I don't know how to be with someone like you."

"Let me show you." He lowers his lips to hers, this time with a little more pressure. His thumb caressing the soft skin behind her ear. When he runs his tongue along the seam of her lips, she elicits a soft moan. "God, Taylor, you keep making noises like that and I don't know how much of a gentleman I'll be able to remain."

"I don't see any problem with that," she whispers, her eyes dark and hooded. "You can be less than a gentleman with me. If you want to."

"You have no idea how much I want to." He places soft kisses along her jaw until she angles her neck to give him better access. "But you deserve to be worshipped, not treated less-than."

Unbidding tears well in her eyes. *Is he for real?* No one has spoken to her this way before. Made her feel like she has worth other than the monetary kind. In the short space of time since meeting Brodie, she's felt more capable and valued than she ever did during her years with Jeremy.

"Hey." His lips brush against her damp eyelids, kissing her tears away. "Are you okay?"

"Mmhmm." She nods, sniffing. "I always cry when a hot guy kisses me. Don't you?"

"Oh, I mean, yeah." He snorts. "I thought it was just me who did that though." He grins, and she chokes out a laugh, swiping at her eyes.

"You're such a dork."

He points to his t-shirt with a picture of a Christmas tree and the words *You look tree-mendous this Christmas.* "I don't think that was ever up for debate."

She eyes the way the shirt clings to his biceps. "You do wear it well though."

"Yes." He pumps his fist. "It's working."

"What is?"

"I buy all my tops two sizes too small so they make me look buff." He flexes, the muscles jumping beneath the cotton.

Taylor rolls her eyes. "You are something else."

"Thanks." He beams, and his eyes light up, tiny creases forming in the corners.

She sighs, dropping her head into her hands. "I'm sorry. I totally ruined the moment, didn't I?"

He shrugs. "Some would say it was I who ruined the moment by making you cry with my hotness."

She snorts out a laugh. "Alright, if you want to take the blame, I'll allow it."

"Good, because I'm taking it regardless." He eyes her. "See? I can be a bad boy."

"Totally."

Chapter fourteen

"Okay, ladies and gentleman." Brodie nods at Byron. "Let's get into our Christmas decorations, shall we?" He has on another Christmas t-shirt, this time with a picture of Yoda saying *Christmas, it is. Merry, it will be.*

He holds up a sheet of paper. "In my hand and on your tables, you'll find a sheet with some ideas, but as per usual, feel free to let your creativity guide you and take you on a journey."

"I like that, eh? Let it take you on a journey." Byron smiles, stretching his long legs out in front of him. "That's what it's all about, right? The journey?"

"Absolutely." Brodie's eyes find Taylor's. "It's all about the journey of life."

Lynette glances between the two as they grin at each other. "Okay." She drags the word out. "You two are being weird." Her lips form an O shape, and she clamps her hand across her mouth. "Oh-em-gee, you did not!" she squeals, latching onto Taylor's arm.

"What?" She looks at her friend with confusion, but realisation sets in when she sees the glint in Lynette's eyes. "Nope." She shakes her head. "We are not discussing this here."

"Oh my God, you did!" She dances in her seat, and from the corner of her eye, Taylor can see Brodie shaking his head, a smirk on his face as he continues talking to the class.

"No, we didn't," she hisses. "At least, not what you think." She gives her friend the side-eye. "I'll tell you later. Focus."

"—thread station here, and then over here we have some little pom-poms and wooden beads that can be threaded on like a strand of tinsel. Any questions?" Brodie glances around the room, his gaze deliberately avoiding Lynette.

Her hand shoots up. "I have a question."

Taylor slaps her hand down. "No, she doesn't."

"I also have a question." Dom raises her hand.

"Yes?"

"What was Lynette going to ask that you're so desperate to keep quiet?" She shoots Taylor a mischievous look then shifts her eyes to Brodie.

"Well—"

Taylor clamps her hand over Lynette's mouth. "Nothing. She wasn't going to ask anything."

Lynette pokes her tongue between her lips and licks Taylor's hand.

"Ugh, gross."

"If you don't want it licked, you shouldn't put it near my mouth."

Byron clears his throat, squirming in his seat, while Taylor wipes her hand down the front of her jeans.

"I have a question," Helen pipes up. "How many Christmas t-shirts do you own? Because by my count, you've had a different one on every time I've seen you, and I've seen you a lot, my boy."

Brodie chuckles. "You know, I don't know the exact number, but somewhere around twelve or thirteen." He shrugs. "I get a new one or three every year and keep adding to the collection."

"A mighty fine collection it is too. We could do with more Christmas spirit around here."

"Well, you've come to the right place then." Brodie draws the attention back to the front of the room by holding up a handmade Christmas tree and a bauble. "Here are some I prepared earlier to give you an idea. I've gone for a natural, rustic look with the tree, and a brighter look for the bauble. If you don't want to use thread like mine, we also have some hessian tape and velvet ribbon you could use instead." He lets his arms drop to his sides. "And away you go."

Lynette picks up where she left off. "You didn't even hesitate when I said we were coming here today, and you've barely said two words to me all week—not even to ask me how it went with Jason—it was phenomenal, by the way. And today you're even sporting a Christmas tee, and you haven't been in the Christmas spirit since…" She lowers her voice, "… you know who."

"Are you complaining that I'm trying to get into the spirit of the season? You? Mrs let's-put-up-our-Christmas-tree-in-November?"

Lynette snorts. "Christmas brings me joy, and I like to make it last. Is that a crime?"

"I never said it was, but I'm sure it is somewhere. But no, I mean that it's odd you're picking my wearing a seasonal t-shirt as a point of contention."

Lynette narrows her eyes. "Stop deflecting. That wasn't my point, and you know it."

Taylor lets out an exasperated sigh. "*Fine.*" She leans in close, so only Lynette can hear. "We kissed. A couple of times. But that's all."

Lynette whoops, practically leaping out of her seat. "Yeeeeessssss, boo. I knew you had it in you."

Taylor scoffs. "Of course I do. It's not like I'm celibate."

"That's debateable."

"Not intentionally."

"Again, that's debateable."

"Ugh, whatever."

"So?"

"So what?"

Lynette rolls her eyes. "How do you find the circumference of a circle... What do you think? How was it?" She says each word pointedly and with a raised brow.

Taylor's cheeks flush, and she brushes a strand of hair behind her ear. "It was nice."

Lynette rears back. "Ugh. That bad?"

Taylor chuckles. "No, there was nothing ugh about it. It was soft, gentle." She touches the pad of her fingers against her lips. "It was nice."

Lynette still looks horrified. "I mean, okay. If that's what floats your boat, then you do you, boo."

"I think it might… *float my boat*." She snickers, burying her face in her hands.

A slow smile spreads across her friend's face. "Aww, Tay. You like, like him like him, don't you?"

"I might."

"That's great, because that man is obviously smitten with you too."

"I hope so." She swallows the lump in her throat, and Lynette wraps an arm around her shoulders.

"He's one of the good ones. You can trust him." She plants a kiss on the side of Taylor's head. "And…" She draws the word out. "If he turns out to be a shithead and hurts you, then I'll tear him limb from limb and bury him nine feet under."

"I think you mean six feet."

"Nope. Nine feet, because you need a layer of concrete to hide the smell, and a dead animal three feet above that. That way when the sniffer dogs scent a body, they'll find the animal and won't keep looking." She taps the side of her head. "I've been thinking about this a lot."

"About how you'll get away with murder?"

"Mmhmm, and who's on my shit list. Brodie's not on there, but he can be. You just say the word."

"Umm, I seem to recall you trying to push us together in the first place." She taps a finger to her chin. "Or am I mistaken?"

"No, you're not mistaken. Like I said, I like the guy and I think you two will make beautiful babies. But the offer is there if it all goes pear-shaped." She juts her chin. "Whatever happens, I got you."

"Well, I appreciate that, even if it *is* a little extreme." Taylor chuckles.

"Are you telling me you wouldn't do the same for me?" She presses a hand to her chest. "And you call yourself a best friend." She tuts.

"Hey, I am there for you one hundred percent, but I have to draw the line at burying a body. You know I'm squeamish."

Lynette folds her arms across her chest. "I at least hope you'll slash some tyres or something."

"Now that I can do." She grins.

"How're we getting on, ladies?" Brodie steps between them, one hand on the back of either chair.

"We're getting on great." Lynette beams up at him. "I think I'll make something *au naturelle*." Her voice takes on a suggestive note. "Nude, if you will."

"Okay." Brodie draws out the word, his cheeks colouring as he scratches the back of his neck. "And you, Taylor?"

"Oh um." She fumbles with the sheet of paper. She'd barely been paying attention as Lynette grilled her. "I'm still deciding."

"Perhaps a fluffy bauble for Atticus?" he suggests, and she grins.

"I love that idea."

"Great." He holds her gaze for a beat before moving to the next table.

"I *love* that idea," Lynette mimics, laughing. "You're so done for."

Chapter fifteen

"Coming!" Taylor calls as she runs down the hall to the front door. She's been deep in the writing trenches for the past few hours, and it was only Atticus digging his claws into her lap that alerted her to the knocking. Who needs a guard dog when you have an antsy cat?

She flings the door open wide, expecting to see a courier, but instead finds Brodie standing there with two grocery bags in his arms and a sheepish grin on his face.

"Hi."

"Hi. I hope you don't mind me swinging by unannounced like this. I was just picking up a few things for dinner, and I think the dance studio must've finished up for the day, because hordes of mums and tiny princesses came in all in one go." He holds the bags up. "You can probably guess what happened."

Taylor laughs. "Panic buying again?"

"Guilty. I bought far too much for just me, so I thought I'd see if you were hungry. Maybe I could cook you dinner?"

"This is becoming a habit of yours; buying too much food." She folds her arms across her chest with a smirk.

"I know. It's a real problem." He grins. "Sooo? How about it?"

She purses her lips and glances over her shoulder. "Umm."

His face drops. "You have plans. Sorry. I should've asked before showing up." He turns. "I'll leave you to it."

"No, wait." She steps out onto the porch, reaching a hand towards him. "I don't have plans. I was just writing. I'm at the business end of it now."

"And I've broken your concentration."

"It's fine, really."

"How about this. You need sustenance to get the book done, right? I'm guessing if you've been down the rabbit hole you won't have eaten much today?"

She scrunches her nose. "I think I had a muesli bar around ten. And bucketloads of coffee."

He glances at his watch. "It's five-thirty. How are you not hangry by now?"

Her stomach chooses that moment to rumble. Loudly.

"I think my stomach has been slowly digesting my internal organs."

"Well, we can't have that. Why don't you let me cook you dinner? You can keep on writing while you're in the zone, and I'll let you know when it's ready."

"I couldn't ask you to do that."

"Ah, well, it's a good thing you didn't ask then, isn't it? I'm offering." He holds the bags up again. "And I have plenty."

Her stomach groans again. "I think you have your answer."

"Great." He steps inside, slipping past her and heading straight into the kitchen. "Off you go. I'll sing out if I need anything."

"Um, okay?" It comes out as a question, but he just waves her on.

"Shoo."

She chuckles, padding back down the hall to her office. It is surprisingly easy to jump back in where she was, even with the hubbub coming from the kitchen. It's been an age since she's had anyone other than Lynette in her kitchen, let alone cooking a meal for her. And rather than it feeling awkward, it feels normal, like it happens on a regular basis.

Brushing those thoughts aside, she dives into her work, her fingers flying across the keyboard as she reaches the crescendo of the story. She'd forgotten how good it feels to get into the flow of writing. The past few years have felt like a struggle, so much so, she'd considered packing it all in after this one. Her three-book deal is about to expire, and while Pam has been hounding her to re-sign, she's been hesitant. With this newfound confidence in herself and finally finding her writing mojo again, that offer might be worth considering.

Before long, the smell of roasting potatoes and garlic wafts down the hall, and it takes all her willpower to stay the course and not follow her nose.

There's a light tap on the door and Brodie pokes his head around. "Hey, hi, sorry to disturb you," he whispers. "But dinner is ready. Would you like me to bring you a plate?"

This guy.

"No, don't be silly. I'll come and join you."

"Are you sure? You look pretty busy, and I promised not to get in your way."

"You also promised to feed me, not wait on me." She puts her screen to sleep. "And anyway, my eyes are going square. I need a break."

"Well, if you insist." He steps aside, swinging the door wide, and sweeping his arm in an arc. "M'lady."

"Why thank you, kind sir." She curtsies, then breezes past him towards the delicious fragrances permeating her house. "It smells amazing."

"Let's hope it tastes amazing too." He pulls out a chair for her, then lights the candle in the centre of the table.

"You brought candles?" She quirks a brow at him.

"Ah, no." He winces. "I found it tucked in one of the kitchen drawers and thought I'd pull it out for ambience. Is that okay?"

She waves him off. "Of course. I didn't even know I had any candles."

Brodie scoots behind the counter, lifting tin foil from the two chicken breasts resting on a chopping board. He grabs her carving knife and sharpens it like a pro.

Once the chicken is sliced, he slides them onto two plates, with buttery corn, green beans, and crisp roast potatoes. He then pulls a loaf of garlic bread from the oven and places it on a small chopping board.

"I hope you're hungry."

She inhales deeply. "Starving."

"Great." He deftly carries both plates on one arm and the chopping board in the other to the table, placing them down one-by-one. "Bon Appetit."

"Well this certainly beats the leftovers I was likely going to eat." Her gaze meets his. "Thank you."

His cheeks flush, and the corners of his mouth twitch. "It's nothing."

"It's not nothing. It's lovely. I don't think a man has ever cooked for me before, other than my father."

Brodie snorts, then catches himself when he sees her expression. "You're serious?"

She nods, a frown on her face. "Yeah, unfortunately I am. To be honest, I didn't think there were any men like you out there anymore." She laughs lightly.

"Men like me how?"

"Oh, you know. Sweet and kind, nurturing."

"Taylor, those aren't special traits. They're a part of being a decent human being." He shakes his head, scratching the back of his neck. "What kind of men have been in your life if me being kind is seen as some great feat?"

"Honestly, I haven't had a great run. They were all only looking out for number one, I'm afraid. I was beginning to think my dad was the last of the good ones." She trails a finger around the rim of her glass. "And then along came you."

He reaches across the table, taking her hand in his. "I don't know how any man could treat you less than the astounding woman you are. On behalf of my species, I am truly sorry for how you've been treated. You have my word, I will put you first, always." His eyes search hers. "That is, if you'll let me."

Swallowing the lump in her throat, she nods. "I think I'd like that."

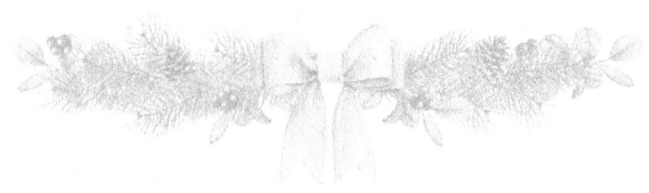

Chapter sixteen

"What exactly is this thing?" Taylor asks as Brodie takes one arm and Lynette takes the other. Both had been adamant she come out with them tonight; some big palooza out front of the library that apparently *everyone* who's anyone goes to.

"God, Tay, have you been living under a rock? It's Light up the Night." Lynette rolls her eyes. "You know, the thing held in town every year with the giant tree and entertainment?"

Taylor stares at her blankly.

"You really have shut yourself away, haven't you?" Brodie says with a frown.

"Tell me about it. I've been trying to drag her out for years. At least now that you two are shacking up I have backup." Lynette winks, and Brodie's eyes widen.

"We're not 'shacking up', Lynny." Taylor shakes her head. "We're... seeing where things go?" She looks to Brodie for confirmation.

"Yeah. It's a little too soon for shacking up. We haven't even been on a real date yet."

Lynette scrunches her nose. "Oh shit, did I crash your date night?" She looks between them both then palms her face. "I did, didn't I? I'm totally the third wheel right now."

"You're not crashing anything." Taylor laughs. "It was your idea to come out in the first place."

"Yeah, but you two are like in the honeymoon phase where you want to spend all your time together, and here I am, getting in the way." She pulls her phone out. "I'll give Jason a call and see what time he knocks off tonight."

"Don't be silly. You don't have to do that. We're not loved-up teenagers who can't keep their hands off each other." Taylor laughs. "We're taking it one day at a time."

Lynette snores. "Where's the fun in that? It's like you skipped the fun part and went straight to being an old married couple." She grabs Taylor's arm. "For the love of God, boo, live a little." She points at Brodie. "That goes for you too. Take the bull by the horns and ride it like there's no tomorrow." She slaps Taylor on the butt. "And by the bull, I mean Taylor. And by the horns, I mean—"

"Oh my God, Lynny, stop!" Taylor laughs, fanning a hand in front of her reddening cheeks. "You're so embarrassing sometimes."

Brodie clears his throat. "I mean, I'm not averse to… riding the bull…" His cheeks flush. "I mean, if that's on the table… and if it's not, that's totally fine too."

"Jesus H Christ, it's like watching a sex scene with your parents in the room – awkward. You two definitely need some alone time, so I'm gonna call Jason and leave you guys to do, or *not do*, whatever you want." She stops walking. "But I sincerely hope you *do* do it. It will be a very merry Christmas for all involved." She winks before sashaying through the throngs of people already gathered. Taylor's chest constricts at the sight of so many milling bodies.

"Well…" Brodie clears his throat again.

"Yup."

"How do you feel about…"

"…Riding the bull?" she finishes.

He chuckles, sliding his palm down his face. "God, that sounds ridiculous, doesn't it? Where does she come up with this stuff?"

She shrugs, laughing. "That's Lynnette for you. She doesn't do things by halves." She slows her pace, nudging him with her elbow. "But, for the record? I'm not averse to it either."

Brodie pauses mid-stride then catches himself, nodding as if deep in thought. "Okay. Good to know. Good to know."

She loops her hand through the crook of his arm. "You're going to be thinking about that all night now, aren't you?"

"Oh, I most definitely will be." He chuckles, only this time it's huskier, and it sets her heart racing.

"I knew there was something going on with you two." Helen strides towards them with a smile from ear to ear. "You make such a striking couple too. You hold onto this one." She nods her head towards Brodie. "He's a keeper, I can tell."

Taylor wraps her arm tighter around his. "I think you might be right," she whispers conspiratorially.

"Helps that he's easy on the eye too, am I right?" Helen whispers back, and they both giggle, heads pressed together. "I certainly wouldn't mind having a gander at him on a daily basis if he were my beau."

"Helen." Brodie presses a palm to his chest. "I had no idea you felt that way. I'm flattered."

"Oh, hush, you. This is girl talk." She tosses him a wink.

"You know—" Taylor pulls away from his grasp and holds her finger and thumb to her chin, gazing at him in appraisal. Tonight, he's sporting a green Christmas t-shirt with a stack of books and the words *All booked for the holidays*, paired with blue jeans and street shoes. "He *is* rather nice to look at, now that you mention it."

"Ladies, please." Brodie fans his face. "You're making me blush."

"Not good with compliments, this one, is he?" Helen hooks a thumb in his direction. "Mind you, I think you're cut from the same cloth, aren't you, Miss Author?" She winks again. "Oh I do wish you'd tell us your nom-de-plume. I'd love to read some of your work."

Taylor's smile falls, and she clears her throat. "I'm not..." She glances at Brodie. "Maybe someday," she says instead, her heart is pounding in her chest at the thought of 'coming out' to everyone all over again.

"Good girl." Helen pats her on the shoulder. "Will we be seeing you at book club next week?"

"Yeah, I think so, though I haven't been doing a lot of reading lately."

"Everyone needs downtime though. You can't work all the time. Even Stephen King says you need to keep reading if you want to write." Helen taps her nose. "And he's one of the greats."

Taylor chuckles. "Yes, I've heard that. I'll try and read something before I see you next."

"Good, good. Well, I best move along and let you two love birds enjoy your evening." She waves then moves off through the crowd.

A screech of interference bursts through the speakers, and there's a collective gasp from around the green.

"Sorry about that, folks. Good evening, everyone, I'm Luke, and I'll be your host on this fine evening. Welcome to Light up the Night!" The crowd applauds. "We have a wonderful lineup for you tonight. First up the melodious tones of our very own Melinda Harper, followed by the kids from All That Jazz doing a few numbers for us, Isabel from the library will be singing a couple of Christmas faves, and, of course, a visit from the big guy himself, Santa!"

The crowd cheers, and children all around them jump and clap.

"Then we'll finish the night off with some fireworks, and one lucky kid out there will get to light the tree!" Another burst of applause. "So, without further ado, can we all give a warm welcome to Melinda!"

"Oh, I love her voice," Brodie says, dragging Taylor towards the front. "She's been singing here the past few years, and we've got her booked in to sing with her sister Sienna at the library the week before Christmas too."

Taylor's jaw tightens. "Know her quite well, do you?" Her words are clipped, and she instantly regrets the way she sounds when Brodie turns to her with an amused look in his eyes.

"No, not really, just through professional channels."

"Oh. Right. Of course." She swallows the bitterness, determined not to let her jealousy ruin the evening. They haven't even sealed the deal, and here she is letting the green-eyed monster rear its ugly head. Off to a great start.

"Come on. Let's have a dance." He takes her hand, walking backwards.

"What? Here? In front of all these people?" Her head swivels side-to-side, taking in the large crowd now congregating on the green.

Brodie laughs. "Yes here. Where else?" He gives her arm a tug until she's directly in front of him. Lifting her hand, he places it on his shoulder, then scoops his arm beneath hers and draws her in close. "Close your eyes and ignore all the people. There's no one here but you and me," he says into her ear.

She does as he says, pressing her cheek to his chest and letting him guide her around the space while Melinda croons softly in the background. All other sounds fade away.

When the song comes to an end, Brodie leads her into a slow spin and then lowers her into a dip. He plants a soft kiss to the tip of her nose then pulls her back up.

The chaos around them floods back in, but it's not as cloying with him by her side. Breathing isn't so hard, and her chest is a little lighter.

"Was that okay?" he asks, his eyes searching hers.

"Yeah, it was." She stands on tiptoes, brushing her lips against his. "Thank you."

"What for?"

"For making this bearable."

"Are you really that uncomfortable?" His brow furrows.

She purses her lips. "No. I thought I would be, but you make it easier."

His chest puffs out, and he stands a little taller. "I'm glad." He draws her into his side, and she nestles in under his arm. "Fancy a bite to eat?"

"I thought you'd never ask."

Chapter seventeen

"What've you got there?" Brodie asks as Taylor joins him on the couch with a large stack of papers and a pen. She lies at one end, and he lifts her feet to his lap, gently kneading the tender flesh.

"My manuscript," she says meekly. "I'm doing a final edit before sending to my agent."

"You finished it?" He beams at her as she nods. "That's awesome, Taylor, I'm so proud of you."

She smiles. "Thanks. I'm proud of me too. There was a moment there where I didn't think I'd get it done in time, but…" She waves the manuscript in the air. "I did it."

He eyes the pages thoughtfully. "You can say no if you want to, and I'll understand, but if I promise not to make it weird… can I read it? Or some of it? I'd love to see what you do."

Her forehead wrinkles and she worries her bottom lip as she tries to form an answer.

"It's okay. You don't have to show me. I know writing is a personal thing." He continues kneading the arch of her foot, but she can tell she's upset him by the set of his jaw. And really, why is she holding back? He's been nothing but kind to her, never given her any reason to doubt him, and he'd been the calm amongst the storm in the crowds over the weekend. There is no reason to hold back any longer. If she wants him in her life, she needs to let him in.

She lifts the resting foot and nudges his thigh. "Let me edit the first chapter, then you can read it. Okay?"

"You don't have to—"

"I know I don't. I *want* you to read it." And as the words leave her mouth, she realises how true they are. She *does* want to share this part of herself with him.

"Really?" His smile is so full of hope and admiration, and her heart gives a tiny flutter.

"Really."

He gives her foot a squeeze, then pulls an imaginary zip across his lips. "I'll let you focus."

She turns her attention back to the papers in front of her, her trusty red pen at the ready to make any changes necessary as she reads.

When she finishes the last page of chapter one, she unclips it from her stack and hands them to him. He takes hold, cradling them in reverence. "Are you sure?"

Her chest flutters again, but she nods. "Yes." Then she focuses on her manuscript again, unsure she can bear watching him read her work. A million thoughts race through her mind.

What if he hates it?

What if he finds flaws?

What if it changes how he feels about her?

What if he turns out to be another Jeremy?

"Oh my God." He looks up, his hands dropping on top of her feet. "I know these characters."

She blinks, her heart pounding. "You do?" She swallows, her throat suddenly thick.

He nods. "Yeah, I do. You're Malorie Hawk, aren't you?"

"You've read my books?" she squeaks, her face warming under his gaze.

"Are you kidding? I've read every single one of them. I bought the special edition copies too for shelf trophies. You're one of my favourite authors." His eyes are wide, and he sweeps a hand through his hair. "This is…" He laughs. "I can't believe it."

"That's me," she says with a shrug. "Surprise."

"This is just…" He scratches his jaw. "Wow. I mean… wow." He turns to her. "You have got to tell book club who you are. Half of them have read your books already. They'll get such a kick out of knowing a famous author."

"I'm not famous."

"You are."

"I'm not. I'm just me. I have no desire to be in the limelight. I only want to write. Fame is not something I've ever sought."

"I get it but not wanting it doesn't make it so. Whether you like it or not, you're one hundred percent famous." He shakes his head. "I know a famous author."

"You know an author. Period."

"Sorry, I don't mean to go on. This is a lot to process. I've kissed Malorie Hawk. I'm massaging the feet of *the* Malorie Hawk." He chuckles. "This is wild."

"*She* is Malorie Hawk." She points to the manuscript still on his lap. "*I* am plain old Taylor."

"You're one and the same though."

"Yes and no. Malorie is the author who hides away in her office and doesn't like people. Taylor is the person in front of you, trying to find her way back to the world she left behind."

He meets her gaze, and while his elation simmers beneath the surface, he seems to understand. "Right. I promised I wouldn't make it weird, and here I am, weirding it out all over the place. I'm sorry."

Her shoulders loosen from around her ears, and she lets out a light laugh. "It's okay. I get it's a shock, but I really hope it doesn't change things between us." She stares at him intently, and he takes the manuscript from her, placing it on her lap, then takes hold of her hands.

"Of course it doesn't."

She lets out a sigh of relief. He's not another Jeremy.

"Can I ask a question?"

"Fire away."

"Where did Malorie come from?"

She smiles. "It's twofold. My grandmother's name was Malory, so it's a nod to her. But my name is Taylor

Marie, so it's a mix of my first names and a shortened version of my real last name, Hawkins. Malorie Hawk."

"Huh. So it's not one of those 'your first pet's name' or 'the street where you live' type of names?"

She laughs. "Ah, no. I'm pretty sure that gives you your stripper name, not author name."

He clicks his finger. "That's right. I'm Cinnamon Porter, by the way. Cinnamon was our cat when I was little."

"How do you do? I'm Fluffy Albert." She cups her hands around her mouth and whispers so Atticus can't hear, "Also my childhood cat."

"Nice to make your acquaintance." He shakes her hand with a mischievous grin. "So, do we strip now or later?" His hips gyrate beneath her feet, and he starts humming the tune of *You can leave your hat on* by Joe Cocker.

She swats at his shoulder with her manuscript, a wide grin across her face. "You're incorrigible. Do you want to read this or not?"

"Right, yes. I do. As you were." He rolls his hand in the air. "Pretend I'm not even here."

Chapter eighteen

Taylor tries to focus on the article she's reading, while Brodie sits beside her, engrossed in her manuscript. It's been three days since she showed him the first chapter and finished her edits, and he's been pestering her ever since to read the rest. She'd put it off long enough, and after he cooked another delicious meal for her, she finally acquiesced.

The only sounds are the slow turning of pages as he reads, and the rushing thrum of her blood pumping through her veins. She's never had anyone read her work in front of her before, not even Lynette. And Pam only ever reads her work when she's sent it. This is a feeling like no other. She's equal parts nauseous and giddy with excitement.

"Well?" she asks when she can wait no longer.

He holds up a finger, his eyes darting back and forth across the page. "Hang on."

She tosses the magazine to the side, unable to focus on anything. Pulling her knees to her chest, she tugs her t-shirt over them and rests her head on top, wrapping her arms around her legs.

"I can feel you watching me."

"I'm not watching you." She shifts her gaze to her toes before glancing back up at him, her bottom lip pulled between her teeth.

He tears his eyes away from the manuscript. "I know you're waiting to hear what I think, but I told you, you're one of my favourite authors. I want to savour this and give it the time it deserves. I can't read with you watching me."

She sighs, even though what he said is actually kind of cute. "Sorry. Patience is not a virtue I learned to cultivate, much to my English teacher's chagrin." She uncoils herself then stands, reaching her hands over her head in a stretch. "I'll go and make some coffee. Want one?"

"Mmm, please." His focus has shifted back to the manuscript.

She pads through to the kitchen, Atticus weaving in and out between her legs. Picking him up, she nuzzles her head amongst his fur, instantly reducing her fears. Brodie has been reading for two hours and has barely lifted his gaze from the papers, so it can't be bad.

She flicks the jug on and is preparing the mugs when her phone buzzes from the counter. Pam's stern face pops up on the screen, so she swipes and puts it on speaker. "Hello?"

"Taylor, glad I caught you. The manuscript is great. Nice wee twist in there, and I like the way you've lightened the overall mood. It's perfect for a Christmas release. I've sent through one or two notes for you, then I think we're ready to go ahead."

"Oh great." A weight lifts from her chest and Taylor takes her first full breath in what feels like days.

"Have you thought about the release and what you want to do? I've got several places who'd like to have you in for a signing or a reading perhaps?"

"You know I don't do that, Pam."

She huffs out a breath, and Taylor can picture her rubbing her temples. "I know, but it *is* part of the process.

At some point you're going to have to face the music. Your fans are calling for it."

"Isn't that part of the allure though? I'm like that artist, Banksy. His identity is a mystery, and it makes his artwork even more sought after."

"Hmm, it's not quite the same with books, I'm afraid. Your fans want to get to know you. That's what sells books these days."

"I like my anonymity," she says quietly. "You know that."

Pam sighs. "I do. But I think it's a mistake. Just... have a think about it, okay? And get back to me on my notes so I can get the ball rolling." There's a click and the line goes dead.

Taylor drops her head into her chest. It's not the first time they've had this conversation, but Pam knows what happened with Jeremy. She was there and part of the initial problem until she realised none of it was coming from Taylor herself.

Brodie clears his throat. "I couldn't help overhearing... For what it's worth, I think she's right. As a fan, I can honestly say it's like a dream when you get to meet the person behind the books you love." He leans his shoulder against the doorframe.

She frowns. "I don't like being the focus of attention. It's a vulnerable thing, putting yourself out there for others to judge, and they *do* judge. Harshly."

"They do, and I get that, but simply by releasing a book you're putting yourself out there, aren't you? So why not own it? Show them you're proud of what you do."

"Because." She wraps her arms around her chest, fighting the hot tears building.

"Because why? Help me understand, Taylor." He reaches for her, but she steps back. "Why won't you let people in?"

"Because I'm scared, okay?"

His hands drop to his sides. "Scared of what?"

"Everything." One tear escapes, and she swipes it away with the back of her hand. "That it will change me, that it will change how people see me, how *you* see me when I'm out there for all to see. It changes things, whether I want it to or not, and I don't want things to change." Her lip wobbles as she meets his gaze. "Things are good right now, and I feel like I'm finding my feet again. I can't..." She shakes her head, unable to continue.

"Taylor..."

"Fame changes things. It brings out sides to people you don't want to see. Cruelty, greed…" She sniffs.

"I can't speak for the other people in your life, but it won't change things between us," he says softly. "I promise."

"It might though."

He shakes his head. "It won't." He pauses. "I don't know what you've been through, but I know you've been hurting, and I don't want you to hurt anymore. All I want is for you to be happy and not feel like you have to hide in the shadows. I don't want anything from you other than that." He shrugs, handing her the stack of papers. "Taylor, I spend my days surrounded by some of the greatest writers in the world, and your book is right up there with them. You have this way of reeling the reader in until they can't help but be drawn to the characters." He takes a beat. "What you write means something, and you should be able to shout from the rooftops that you are the person who created this amazing world. I guarantee you that for every critical reviewer out there, there's twice more out there who read your books to escape and find joy. Don't let the words and actions of the few ruin it for the many. Let them see who you are and fall in love with you like I have."

Her head shoots up as his words register. "You've fallen in love with me?"

"I…" He reaches up to rub the back of his neck. "Yeah, I think I have." He meets her gaze with a soft smile. "Is that okay?"

"Because of my writing?" she asks with bated breath.

He chuckles. "Because of *who* you are. Yes, your writing is brilliant, but that's not all you are. That's not why I love you. It's your humour and intelligence, the way you care so much about Atticus. There's so much more to you than what you write."

She chews her lip, unsure how to respond. It's all so much to take in.

He takes a step back, holding his palms out. "I don't expect you to say anything back. I just want you to know that I see you for you, and I know you're scared, but you don't have to be. I'm not going anywhere, and I'll be right by your side whatever you decide."

Chapter nineteen

"I never thought a wizard beard would do it for me, but here I am." Lynette shrugs, taking a large mouthful of wine. "It's a lot softer than you'd think."

"So that's what? Date number four? This sounds like it could be getting serious, Lynny." Taylor waggles her brows at her friend, welcoming the distraction from her conversation with Brodie. It shook her, and she's not entirely sure how she feels about it.

Lynette snorts. "Me and serious do not go together, you know this. It's just a bit of fun." She takes another gulp of her drink then holds her hands out wide like she's sizing a fish. "A *huge* amount of fun."

Tayor pulls the cushion out from behind her and swats her friend. "You're so crass."

"That's why you love me." She grins, but it quickly turns to a frown when she sees the look on Taylor's face. "What's wrong?"

She squinches her eyes closed, pinching the bridge of her nose. "Brodie told me he loves me."

"Get out!" Lynette swings her legs up off the floor to sit cross-legged, waiting for the tea to be spilled. "You have been keeping that one quiet."

Taylor nods, her lips sucked in.

"But that's great, isn't it? Why do you look like your nana just died?" Her eyes search Taylor's. "You don't feel the same?"

"I don't know how I feel." She shrugs. "It's all so sudden. We haven't even known each other that long."

"Stranger things have happened. It's been a month, Tay. Mum and Dad knew within a week that they were it for each other, and they're still going strong."

"I guess…"

Lynette eyes her. "The old you was a romantic at heart who would've been jumping for joy, not acting like they're about to be drawn and quartered. What's this really about?"

"He knows."

"Knows?"

She swallows. "That I'm Malorie. I showed him my manuscript."

Lynette leans back. "Okay, we'll discuss why he got to read it before me later, but if you showed him, then you must've wanted him to know, right? I don't see what the issue is."

"I showed him before he told me how he feels."

"And?" She draws the word out, and Taylor sighs.

"How do I know it's not just because of who I am? He's already tried to convince me to announce it to everyone."

"Tay, he's not Jeremy."

"I know, but—"

"No buts about it. Come on, has he changed the way he's been around you? Aside from telling you how he feels?"

"I mean, no."

"And weren't you feeling all giddy towards him too?"

"Well, yeah."

"So why are you turning this into something it's not?" She sets her glass down, shuffling closer. "You have to let it go. Jeremy is the past. Brodie is the future."

"But what if—"

Lynnette shakes her head. "*If* we're wrong about him, and shit goes down, I already told you what I'll do to him. Nine feet under, remember?" She reaches both hands behind Taylor's neck and pulls her in so their foreheads are pressed together. "I've got you, boo. And if you let him, Brodie will have you too. You can't move forward if you don't let your future outshine your past."

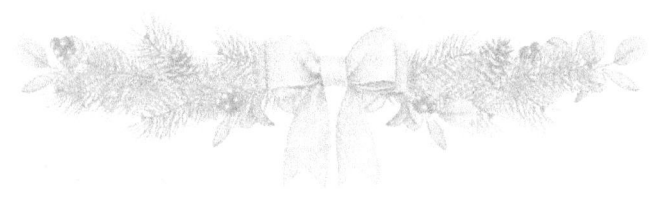

Chapter twenty

"Welcome to book club, everyone. As it's December now, this will be our last one for the year." There's a collective groan from around the group. "But that doesn't mean you can't still pop in and visit me here." Brodie smiles. "And, as a special treat, I brought chocolates!" He pulls a box of Favourites out from behind his back and places it on the book table. "Now, who would like to start us off?"

Butterflies dance in her stomach as Taylor stands, raising her hand. "Um, I would, if that's okay?"

Brodie's head tilts and a small smile forms on his lips. "Sure. Go ahead."

She clears her throat. "Uh, hi, everyone. I'm Taylor, I joined last month."

"We remember you, dear." Vera smiles warmly.

"Yes, and can I say, I love the new colour." Helen points to her head. "Very Christmassy that."

Taylor runs her hands through her now scarlet red hair. "Thank you, Helen. I thought it was time for a change." She beams, but inside her heart is thundering.

"A change is as good as a holiday, they say," Rowena adds.

"Yes, I suppose it is." She shuffles her feet, running her hands down the front of her pants. "Anyway, I only really have one book to share with you this month. It's the only one I've managed to read, and multiple times at that." She catches Lynette's eye, who gives her an encouraging smile. "I don't have it here with me today because it's not quite ready yet, but the book I've been reading is my own one." She pauses a beat. "It's the latest addition to the Clearwater Mysteries series."

"Wait, why does that sound familiar?" Vera asks. "Have I read those?" She thumbs through her notebook.

"*You* might not have, but *I* have." Rowena's eyes shine. "Are you Malorie Hawk then?"

Taylor curtsies. "I am."

"Who's Malorie Hawk when she's at home?" Jocelyn asks.

"Her obviously," Helen remarks. "Keep up."

"Wonderful!" Rowena claps her hands. "I never can guess whodunnit until the very end. Fabulous stories, all of them."

"I have to agree," Helen pipes up. "Fancy that. We're amidst the presence of a famous author." She waves her hand towards Taylor. "Oh, how exciting. I can tell everyone I know *the* Malorie Hawk."

"Are any of us in your book?" Dom asks with a cheeky grin, and Taylor's cheeks flush.

"I may have taken inspiration from a few of you. And, Byron, thank you for passing on that fungi book, it came in very handy for part of the plot."

"Oh, how neat. You're so welcome."

Jai leans forward. "When does it come out?"

"In three weeks. Right before Christmas." Taylor chews her bottom lip, glancing towards Brodie. "And I was thinking that if it's alright with the library, perhaps I could hold my book launch here? Talk to my readers and sign some books?"

A slow smile spreads across his face. "I'm sure that can be arranged." He leans back in his seat, stretching his legs out in front of him. "I believe the Community Librarian is easily persuaded."

"I hear he likes riding bulls." Lynette stifles a laugh unsuccessfully, and Taylor's cheeks redden further.

"I was meaning chocolate, but I'll take a bull ride if that's on offer." He winks at Taylor, and she covers her face with her hands.

"I think I missed something." Helen scratches her head. "Where are the bulls? Are they part of the story?"

"You'll just have to read it and find out, won't you?" Lynette says, waggling her brows. "She can't go giving away all her secrets."

Taylor swats her. "Shush you. I'm not going to make them read the book to find out there are no bulls in there." She turns to Helen. "But I *do* hope you read it anyway, even if it is sans bulls."

"Are you kidding? We'll all be reading it as soon as we can get our hands on it. Mark my words, you'll have your very own fan group with us. Isn't that right?" Rowena looks at each club member, and they all nod in agreeance. "I'm afraid you'll be stuck with us for the long haul now."

Warmth floods her chest. "I'm glad to hear it." She takes a deep breath, then crosses the circle to where

Brodie sits. "I have one other secret to share," she says quietly, ducking her chin.

Brodie sits forward, and with two fingers beneath her chin, tilts her head to meet his gaze. "I'm listening."

"I should've said it the other night, but I was overwhelmed and a little wary, to be honest." She glances over her shoulder at Lynette. "But I've had time to think and digest it all, and you were right. It's time I let go of the past and start letting people back into my life. But I'm going to need your help, if you're still willing?"

He palms her cheek, his thumb stroking back and forth. "Of course I am. I meant what I said, Taylor. I love you, and I will be there for you in any way you need me."

"Good, because—" she clears her throat, "—love you, I do," she says in her best Yoda impression.

He snorts out a laugh. "You do?"

"I do." She nods, pushing up on tip toes to brush her lips against his.

"Alright, folks." Lynette steps in front of them, blocking their embrace from view. "Nothing to see here. Jai, what did you read this month?"

Epilogue

"Welcome everyone to the official book launch of the latest Clearwater Mysteries book, Once Upon a Mushroom written by a local lass who I believe is a member of the library book club, is that right?" Luke looks to Brodie, who gives the thumbs up. "Indeed, she is. Now this is her first time out in public as an author, even though she already has a whopping eight books under her belt, and this makes nine."

"You ready?" Lynette whispers as she takes her seat next to Taylor, giving her hand a squeeze.

"Too late if I'm not," she whispers back.

"So, without further ado, let's bring her up to the front, Miss Malorie Hawk!" Luke holds his hand out, palm up, as Taylor stands from in the crowd and makes her way to the front.

He hands her the mic, and she thanks him.

"Hi, everyone." She waves. "As Luke said, I am Malorie Hawk, and I'm the author behind the Clearwater Mysteries series."

She talks about the series and where the idea came from for the small-town detectives she writes about, then gives a brief overview of the new book before reading a snippet from the first chapter.

"Wowsers, hooked from the first chapter, am I right?" Luke says, miming catching a fish on a line.

"Well, thank you, Luke. I do like to grab people as early into the piece as I can."

Lynette snorts. "Some might say she likes to grab them by the horns."

Taylor shakes her head, trying to ignore her giggling best friend in the audience.

"You certainly grabbed my attention. And on that topic, how do you know what's going to grab people and where to even start when it comes to writing a book? You seemed to just jump on in there, right in the thick of it without build up. Is that a strategy of yours?"

"I suppose you could say it is, yes. You want the reader to feel as though they're a part of the story or conversation. Readers are smart, they don't need you to start from the beginning to understand what's going on. And the first few lines can be make or break. You need to capture their attention from the word go, make them want to keep reading."

Luke asks a few more questions before opening it up to the crowd filling the space. A few familiar faces from book club dot the audience, and they're the first to put their hands up and speak. Helen, of course, goes straight for the jugular.

"On a scale of 1 to 10, how spicy is this one?"

"Ooh, I would say a three?" Taylor looks to Lynette, who makes a DeNiro face and tilts her head side-to-side, nudging her thumb in the air. Taylor laughs. "Okay, maybe more of a four. This series is tamer on the spice front." She speaks around the side of her hand, as if divulging a secret. "But if you're looking for a bit of heat, I suggest you check out my other pen name, Remy Shaw."

Brodie's head lowers and he punches something into his phone. With a smile, he holds it aloft. "We have two of them on the shelves right now."

"Be a dear and put one aside for me, would you?"

"Already on it, Helen." Lynette runs to the shelf close by and pulls out a book with a bare-chested, tattooed man on the cover. "Here you go."

"You're an angel."

"How about we mingle and get some books signed?" Luke asks. "And while we do that, we've got the marvellous melodies of Melinda crooning Christmas carols."

Taylor takes her seat behind the table, her pen at the ready. Lynette and Brodie take up their spots on either side of her, each with a stack of books and goodies to give out. She signs until her hand is sore and the group is dwindling.

"That was a roaring success, don't you think?" Lynette plonks herself down beside Taylor. "How many books did you bring again?"

"Fifty."

"And there's only one, two, three, four... five left. That's pretty bloody awesome, if you ask me." She raises a hand, waiting for a high five.

Taylor acquiesces then shakes her hand out, flexing her fingers to loosen them back up again. "Yeah, I'm happy with that." She smiles, her heart full.

"You were amazing up there too," Brodie says. "You didn't seem nervous at all."

"Oh, I was packing myself, believe me."

"No one would've suspected. You're a natural." He plants a kiss to the top of her head. "I'm proud of you."

"I'm proud of me too."

"I'm proud of me also." Lynette stands, gathering the last of the supplies and putting them into the box beneath the table.

Brodie frowns. "Um, why?"

Lynette cocks a hip. "Ah, none of this—" She waves her hand through the air, "—would've happened without me." She flicks her hair. "I set the ball in motion by dragging this one out."

Taylor chuckles. "She does have a point."

"Right, so we're all proud, now let's make like a Christmas tree and get lit."

Acknowledgements

As always, I have to thank Trina for her editing prowess. She always catches the things I miss.

Debs, my writing partner in crime, thanks for motivating me and keeping me company while I write. I always seem to get so much more done when you're around.

Thanks to the Ashburton Library book club, who have always made me feel like I belong and have cheered me on along the way. Your friendship means a lot to me.

Thanks to the Ashburton Library team, who pimp my books out to everyone and also keep me on target by asking me how my books are coming along. You're the best team to work with, and I feel so grateful every day that this is my job.

And, of course, to my readers, who make this possible. I always wanted to write, but I never thought I'd be able to publish a book, let alone the number I have under my belt now.

Love you!

Stacey

About the Author

Stacey Broadbent is from New Zealand. She writes under three different names (Cyan Tayse, Stacey Jayne, Stacey Broadbent) and a variety of genres, so there is something to suit most tastes. Her storytelling style combines wit, relatability, and emotional resonance - inviting readers into the messy, marvellous folds of life.

An avid reader and lover of all things bookish, Stacey has made it her goal to share about her favourite authors and books she's read, while also building her own publishing story. She is a qualified proofreader and has recently completed her Diploma in Library and

Information and is currently working towards a Diploma of Arts.

Her TBR is never-ending, and though she struggles to keep up with it, she continues to add more.

As well as reading, her hobbies include LEGO, cross-stitch, crochet, and diamond art, and you can often find her sharing about her latest project on TikTok and Instagram

If you feel like stalking her, here are the links!

www.staceybroadbent.com/
www.facebook.com/StaceyBroadbentAuthor
www.amazon.com/author/staceybroadbent
Goodreads: https://goo.gl/YJ6dXa
www.instagram.com/authorstaceybroadbent/
www.bookbub.com/authors/stacey-broadbent
www.tiktok.com/@authorstaceybroadbent

Other Books by Stacey

Standalone
Never Judge a Book
Emma
Deep Heat
Lady Luck: A Deep Heat bonus novella
Fever
Broken
Awesome Applesauce

Christmas in New Zealand
A Christmas Tail
A Novel Christmas

A Step in Time series
Dancing through the Storm
Dancing in Circles
Dancing with Destiny
A Step in Time: the complete series

Super Mum series
Frazzled
Frazzled and Frumpy
Frazzled, Frumpy and Fabulous!
Super Mum: the complete series

Dark sins novellas
Sins of the Flesh
Mine

Hellhounds MC
Cut Loose
Break Loose
Let Loose

Short Stories and Poetry
Musings, Mournings, and Misadventures
Musings, Mayhem, and Mystery
Musings, Magic, and Mischief
Musings of a Writer: the complete collection

Anthologies
Scars to your Beautiful
Witching Hour: Vices and Virtues
The White Ribbon Collection
Key to my Heart
A Touch of Inspiration
No Place Like Home
Serendipity
Lucky Star
Hellhounds
The Poetry Project